SEVEN CROWS

Justin Killam

One crow for sorrow,
Two crows for joy,
Three crows a girl,
Four crows a boy,
Five crows for silver,
Six crows for gold,
Seven crows a story,
Never to be told.
– *anonymous folk poem*

Seven Crows
Book I - Preludes and Lamentations

7CROWS.HUNTANDKILLAM.CA

Copyright © Justin Killam, 2013
Apocrypha Studios
APOC.HUNTANDKILLAM@GMAIL.COM

This is a work of fiction. Names, characters, places, and incidents are either the product of the author's imagination or used fictitiously, and any resemblance to actual persons, living or dead, events, or locales is entirely coincidental.

ISBN-13: 978-1491043769
ISBN-10: 1491043768

Cover Design by Damien Hunt
Title Font: IM Fell English
The Fell Types are digitally reproduced by Igino Marini. www.iginomarini.com
Author Photo by Shawn Bourque

First Paperback Edition - Updated [2024]

Seven Crows : 3 : Justin Killam

For Charla;
who loved me when we were just kids,
and loves me still,
even now that I am just a much older kid.

For Jeff and Chuck;
who both have, on numerous occasions, given me swift kicks to the ass when I needed to recognize my potential.

For Clint;
who introduced me to D&D, which set off a chain reaction of events that led to my love (some might say obsession) of gaming, storytelling, and the incredible creativity that comes from mixing both.

For my students;
in which I see greatness, and am inspired,
and -in turn- help me see greatness within myself.

For you, who bought this book;
thank you for your support and helping me start this new journey as an author.

This is only the beginning...

- Prologue -

"Deep down, everyone desires a touch of the tragic. What's most amusing is that many, whether they know it or will admit it, wish for it to befall themselves." – *unknown*

The sun has set, leaving a wake of pink tinged clouds on the horizon followed by an ever deepening purple. The colours of a terrible bruise, not yet healing. I know how that feels. It's how I feel right now.

I stumble through a field of grass grown almost higher than myself, stalks of green and yellow whipping and tangling about me. Grass stains, I imagine them yellowish-green, don't show against the deeper, darker, crimson stains already clinging to my clothes... to my skin. I blunder my way through the field and towards... I have no idea. I don't know or care where I go. No destination in my mind, just the desperate drive to escape.

Everything blurs. Tears flow from eyes stung by thick black smoke. The smoke fills the darkening sky, billowing out from behind me and flowing across the field in all directions. Filling my eyes, it picks and scratches. Filling my lungs, it burns its way in and clutches my chest in a smothering grip. It squeezes, tightens and the world blurs further, begins to spin. I fall to the ground in a tangle of grass.

All goes dark and I welcome the nothingness. It's as good an escape as any.

I wake up sometime later, on my back and staring up at the sky. Thick grass is bunched up beneath me and more of it crowds around me. It frames the churning sky overhead. A mixture of cloud, fog and the black smoke hiding the near night sky above.

I realize that the hideaway must still be burning. It was burning when I escaped, it...

I...

No...

My mind reels backwards to the hideaway, back to earlier that day, back to the others, back to the incident. Memories rush forth. Though my soul rages against it. Though I would do anything to avoid it. Though I would pay any price to not have to relive the horror. To not remember would be Heaven, but such a divine reward is not to be mine. I am undeserving of such, and so it all comes back to me.

I turn over on my side and throw up all over the grass. I heave, trying to empty my churning, bile filled stomach. I empty my guts, but still more needs to be brought up. The memories flash fry their way through my skull, and I try to throw them up onto the grass as well. I stop only after, it seems, everything I have ever consumed has reversed its way through me.

I feel empty, scoured through and through; mind, body and soul. Empty is good. Or -at least- better.

Time to go.

Go, where? It's dark and I can't see the puddle of sick in the grass, so I roll away from where I think it is and pull myself to my feet. I look around, consciously avoiding turning back the way I came. I don't want to spend the night in a field of grass so I start to walk, picking a random direction that still manages to take me farther away from... that place.

Flashing lights, blue and red and more red, appear in the distance and draw me in. After I walk for a while through the deepening dusk, they appear. I go with them, the police, without a fuss.

I'm in the back of a van. It's all comfy and clean inside, even the air is filtered, and it is all very official looking. I could almost worry about making the spotless seats dirty, but truly I just don't give a damn. Especially after all I have just been through.

My mind slips away from such memory-invoking thoughts and I just sit quietly. They make sure the door is locked with a soft click before leaving me with the others.

They are all here, the others, I know it. I don't look at them, I don't need to. They have all survived because it would only be right that all of us suffer to live with what we have done. It would be a blessing if they were dead or gone away so that I don't have to remember. Another blessing that I am not deserving of, and so I know they are all here with me.

We sit in silence, some of us in shame, as the van pulls away from the only home we have ever known; the orphanage. It seems almost as if the van is still and our home is abandoning us as it slides away. Even the dark tinted windows and the coming twilight cannot hide it from our eyes; an old squat building of loose slats, rusted bars over windows of warped closed wood, and yellowed layer over yellowed layer of peeling, once white, paint.

I blink and the memory of the building is

replaced by reality. The orphanage is a pile of black ash and glowing embers, still smoking as the last pockets of fire struggle to keep ablaze in the face of the hard working fire department. I blink again, but the view remains the same. I don't remember it being on fire, but then the last thing I want to do is remember anything, so I turn away.

Our home is gone.

We are taken away and the police men send the others to new homes. They do not get to stay together. They are alone.

Alone is good. Or -at least- better.

The others may not agree with me.

Book I

Preludes and Lamentations

"In the beginning...
All the best stories begin in this way..."
    – *unknown*

- Chapter 1: Sorrow -

"The world doesn't run on kindness, and you should thank whatever's-in-charge for that. Think of the cataclysmic world extinction event that would cause." – *unknown*

❖ 1 ❖

The second time they call out his name he still continues to stare out at the little dirt town called Shaw. He is continuing to ignore them. This is not a good thing to do.

[*Bron...*]

I say nothing else, not wanting to push him. I see the corners of his mouth firm as he presses his lips together. Those clear pale blue eyes of his do flicker once towards me and then off to his right towards the path.

The trees on the back end of Bruknows Hill sway in the wind behind us both, but we can still hear the Goodpaw kids pushing their way through the brush. They will be walking out through the path in only a minute or two.

Bron looks back out over the little town. Barely more than a village and nestled in a small valley in the middle of the mid-northern prairies. No more than a dozen gravel streets off the paved main street, with a grungy poor section of dilapidated trailers on the other side of the tracks.

The valley is pretty much just a sink hole in the flat landscape and the air doesn't move much down there. I know Bron is thinking about just how much it stinks in Shaw. I don't disagree with him.

The third time they call out his name he still doesn't answer or leave his seat, only shifts uncomfortably on the boulder in front of the town's water tower. There is a bit of fear darkening his eyes, but it's overshadowed by his stubbornness.

[*Bron!*] I try his name again, this time louder.

"What!" He shouts back at me, whipping his head around to stare defiantly back at me.

I hiss a warning for silence back at him, [*bad enough you risk their ire by ignoring them, you wish them to think you mad as well?*]

He gives me one of those looks of confused disbelief. They make me uncomfortable.

[*What?*] I ask.

[What does that even mean?] he asks back.

[*What does what mean?*] I ask again, confused.

[Ire, I've never even heard of the word!]

Well, this is awkward.

[*Ah... yes, well it holds the same meaning as anger or rage. You understand?*]

[No, not at all. And why would I care if they think I am angry?]

I sigh. Judging the look in his eyes, the sigh isn't helping my case at all. I try to mend the situation as much as possible. [*Apologies. I used the word mad to mean mentally unstable. As in crazy. Do you understand my concern now?*]

He scowls at me. It is a poor argument coming from an imaginary friend. Especially an imaginary friend using far too complicated a vocabulary for a kid in grade seven to easily follow.

[Chaid, what do you want?] he wearily asks.

At least he's not talking out loud to himself any longer. He is talking -thinking loudly would be the best way to describe it- to me instead of continuing to ignore me.

I try to tone down my vocabulary, even though this often does not work. [*Well, just for starters, not to watch you beaten into unconsciousness by those cretins. Tell me, is this not a reasonable request?*]

Silence is his answer, accompanied by a cold stare. I'm not getting through that barrier of stubbornness, only adding to its strength. Bron turns back to stare out over the town. I sigh and turn to watch the path.

Right on cue, the Goodpaw kids emerge from the back woods. They glare right through me and at the back of Bron's head. I'd say I have a couple minutes, tops, before they arrive to menace him.

They disappear behind the last hill before reaching the top of Bruknows and I turn back towards Bron, brooding on his boulder. There is a far away look in his eyes. His mouth parts slightly, as if he is about to speak, but then closes quietly once more.

[Chaid...] he starts, but then pauses to figure out just how to say what he wants to say, [you're never there in my dreams, not that I can see anyway... why is that?]

This question is... unexpected. He continues to stare off into the distance without looking at me. I am thankful that I have his attention, but the oddity of his question has me stumped for a moment.

[*I do not know. If you are asking me if I can spy into your dreams without you knowing, the answer is no. I am not privy to your dreams or secret thoughts or anything you do not wish to share with me, Bron.*]

He still does not turn to look at me, but there is a flicker at the edges of my vision when I mention sharing. Like a strip of pre-digital film slipping over my eyes. I see something darkly red and flickering, but it is gone before I can see it in any detail. I am pretty sure it came from Bron, like a broadcast of what he is seeing in his mind.

His lips, already pressed together tightly enough to make them a bloodless pale, press more firmly together as he struggles with something. It is like he wants to share with me, but is afraid.

Afraid of me? Afraid of my reaction? Afraid of what it might mean? Afraid of...

No, Bron is not afraid of me or my judgments. They are many and harsh, my judgements, but never for Bron. He judges himself too harshly enough already, without me to add to the burden. Then it hits me. He doesn't want to confide in me because he is afraid of how he will judge himself.

I sigh once again. It's not an easy job, being Bron's only true friend. I start to say something, but he beats me to the punch.

[Chaid?] he says.

He is standing up, looking down at the base of Bruknows Hill. His eyes are troubled.

[Who is...]

He finishes the thought out loud, saying, "Is that guy watching us?"

I turn to look down the hill and catch a glimpse of a limo parked by the side of the dirt road. It's a service road for the water tower perched at the top of Bruknows Hill, and goes nowhere else, so why would a limo be there? Before I can study the figure standing next to the limo there is a shout behind me.

"Moron!"

The Goodpaw kids crest the final hill, reaching the top of Bruknows. They pass right through me on their way to Bron. They don't yell his name a fourth time, but resort to insults.

Typical. Typical and indicative of Bron being bruised within moments.

"Hey moron, you finally go full basket case or what?"

That's Marten, the oldest. Tall and lean, he could be athletic if he didn't sit on his ass all day doing nothing. He is supposed to be in high school, but ask him about it and he will give you a sob story about how his family needs him out of school and working to support the family. How he is supporting them by sitting around watching pathetic daytime reality TV all day is beyond me. His face is a collection of lean angles, tan skin, and eyes that looked like they once held a glimmer of spirit. Even now, when he is pissed and ready to pound someone, they just look... tired.

"Jeez Bron, kill ya to answer back? It's not like we can't just leave your ass behind, ya know."

That's Niles, whom I have labelled the gateway friend. Bron hates it when I call him that. Niles is the same age as Bron and they are both in the same grade seven class at school. It is easier to deal with daily doses of bullying when someone else is going through the same crap and occasionally they can stand up for each other. I get that, but what I don't get is why Bron wants to put up with Niles and his jerk-wad brothers bullying him after school. I keep telling Bron he would be better off with just me.

Niles looks like a miniature version of his older brother, except for his eyes. They are not as tired as his brothers. Niles still talks about what he wants to do when he gets out of Shaw. Well, he talks about it when Marten is not around.

"Hey guys, sorry I didn't hear you." Bron smiles, a little goofily like he is embarrassed, and points down the hill. "I was just watching this idiot get lost down..."

I don't get a chance to applaud Bron's tactical attempt to refocus their attention away from himself. Marten's hand flashes out and the backhands Bron across the side of the face.

If I were real, the sound of knuckles cracking as I clench my fists in helpless rage would echo all over this wretched town.

Marten grins, a bit too eagerly, at the sharp crack. "You heard that though, right moron?"

Bron turns back towards Marten, holding his reddening face in his hand and trying not to show the water building in his eyes. He doesn't respond.

Marten glances behind Bron and, right on cue, Niles gives him a rough shove from behind.

The boulder is not all that big to fall from, but this side of the Bruknows is steep and strewn with large rocks. At the bottom of the hill, the only thing stopping anyone from tumbling into the ditch is a jagged barbed wire fence. Bron falls and tumbles, but luckily recovers before he can fall too far or get seriously hurt.

The youngest Goodpaw, Teddy, joins his older brothers as they watch Bron take a tumble. He doesn't say much, not ever. Right now he isn't laughing along with or even sharing the same disappointed look that his brothers have as Bron starts to climb back up from not too far down the hill. Teddy is in grade five and still knows how to smile without it being aimed at someone being tormented. I wonder how long it will be until he starts to get that same worn look as the rest of the Goodpaws. Then I see Bron regain the top of the hill and start to check himself for bruises and I find I don't really care what happens to any of the Goodpaws, even Teddy.

[*I would dance upon their graves, each and every one of them, and laugh merrily at their demise. The more horrid the death, the louder I would laugh.*]

I probably shouldn't have said that.

Bron dusts himself off and casts me a sour look that tells me that he heard my rant and disapproves. Then he puts firmly in place that goofy smile, like they are all just playing around.

"Good one guys, where are we going?" He asks like the good chum he is.

Teddy chimes in before his brothers can, a smile upon his face. "The beaver dam! They are working on it again and I want to see how big it is getting."

Marten and Niles both roll their eyes, but they

do turn away from Bron and start heading back into the woods behind the hill. Bron joins them, trying to hide a slight limp. Everything is right as rain.

I want to puke. I want to scream at Bron to just take off and... do what? His foster parents are just as bad, just as abusive.

I want...

What I really want is to be able to offer Bron an alternative that is actually better than what he currently has to put up with. But I have nothing... for now.

❖ 2 ❖

The beaver dam is an impressive sight to a bunch of kids. It might be an impressive sight to a bunch of anyone. It rises out of the middle of the swamplands at the lowest end of the Shaw valley. It varies in size with each year, depending on how many beavers there are. This year there are a couple of them visible, bringing sticks and mud to patch up their home. The bundle rises out of the pond a good four or five feet.

Bron always seems to take an interest in the never ending construction, but I just don't see the point. It sits in the middle of a pond, not even damming anything. Every year when summer starts, the high school kids pelt it with cherry bombs and firecrackers. One year they tried to burn it down, but beavers can be pretty fierce when protecting their home and one kid lost a toe. Marten always points out that kid in town, getting a laugh from "Toeless" limping down the sidewalk.

Teddy and Bron find a good place to sit and

watch. They talk about what the beavers have done to the dam already this year and predict what else they will do. Niles and Marten forage the area for rocks and stones that they can toss at the beavers to watch them scatter.

Nobody notices the other kid at first. The swamplands border on the new, but most likely forever stalled and never to be finished, Shaw housing project. To make sure the swamp didn't flood the new building site, the town built a large hill along the edge of the swamp. It's a good fifteen feet high, a steep pile of jagged rock and dirt, overgrown with weeds. Standing atop this hill is a teen, scowling down at us.

He looks like a high school freshman. Marten notices him after a moment and flips him the finger and tells him where to go. The kid disappears behind the steep hill.

No big deal. Niles and Marten go back to their collecting, adding to their small pile of stones. Teddy continues to describe what kind of structure he would create if he were a beaver. Bron listens, but also glances over his shoulder a couple of times. I know he is checking to see if the high schooler has come back. I can't blame him for his paranoia.

A few minutes later I scowl.

[*Bron, we have more company.*]

Bron looks towards me and then follows my pointing finger. He scowls as well.

There are more teens atop of the hill, looking down at the Goodpaws and Bron with cold smiles on their faces. There are only three of them, but they are bigger than even Marten. Shaw is a proud farming community, and these three could be on the welcome billboard at the edge of town.

[Crap, what do they want?]

Before the Goodpaws notice, or Bron can give them a heads up, one of the high schoolers starts yelling at Marten.

[*It appears they want Marten. Bron...*]

He looks over at me, giving me a dark stare, but I can see the worry in his eyes. I wonder, for a quick moment, if he can see worry in my eyes.

[*...do not get involved. Do not stand up for the Goodpaws, they would not stand up for you. Just take care of yourself, Bron. Please...*]

The back and forth barrage of insults between the eldest Goodpaw kids and three high school farm giants continues to intensify. Curses have turned into threats of violence.

Bron doesn't answer me, but gets up and pulls Teddy away from his brothers, who don't even seem to care about their youngest brother at the moment. In getting ready to torment the beavers, they have already collected a nice pile of stones. It's Marten, and in this I am not the least surprised, who tosses the first stone.

The stone sails through the air, and comes nowhere even close to hitting either of the three on top of the hill, but that doesn't stop them from being outraged. This has just gotten physical. Niles follows suit and starts tossing stones. The three teens yell back and duck flying rocks for a few moments before retreating down the other side of the steep hill and disappearing.

All four of us share a moment of tension in the silent aftermath of the confrontation. I sigh in relief and note that Bron does the same. Marten shatters the quiet with a loud laugh. It sounds like a lame dog with a smoker's bark. Niles joins in, Teddy a moment later, and even Bron joins in celebrating their victory with a forced smile.

"You're all going to die!"

I look up expecting tragedy and, unfortunately, am not mistaken in this assumption. The Goodpaws shut up and Bron's smile fades completely as all eyes look to the top of the hill. The three high schoolers have already returned, and they are not alone. I don't count all of them, but I estimate a couple dozen.

They are spread out along the top of the ridge-like hill, grinning and leering down at us. Every one of them is holding a baseball bat or hockey stick.

They came prepared.

They had this well planned.

We are all in a lot of trouble.

Marten, never one to back down or even attempt to resolve things peacefully, picks up another stone and tosses it. It hits the one who just yelled down at us, dead centre of his forehead. He disappears as he collapses behind the steep hill.

[*Oh brilliant...*]

Marten, grinning triumphantly yells up at them, "Turn around and get the hell out of here or you'll all get the same!"

[Oh crap...]

[*Bron...*]

There is a moment of thick tense silence. I

notice out of the corner of my eye that even the beavers have stopped their work and are sitting atop their dam, watching to see how this all plays out.

[*...run.*]

One of the kids at the top of the hill, his face all red with anger, screams, "kill em!'

Not, I note, a "get em," but a fully enraged and committed "kill em."

[*RUN BRON!*]

Marten, ever the gallant ass, turns and runs without saying a word. Niles at least yells at Teddy to run and pushes his younger brother ahead of himself. Bron follows behind as the four of them run for the maze of wood paths that lead back to Bruknows hill. I turn and watch the gang of crazed high schoolers charge down the steep hill, screaming and waving their bats and sticks like a pack of bloodthirsty wolves on the scent of fresh prey. Most of them fall, which would be funny if I wasn't so worried about Bron, but it does slow down the gang and give Bron and the Goodpaws a head start.

This is messed up. The Shaw bullying scene has always been fierce with name calling, pushing and shoving, and minor bruises, but no one has ever been hospitalized before. The looks on the faces of the high schoolers is frightening, like hospitalization is the least of what they are aiming for. A vision of Bron laid out, pale and unmoving, on a morgue slab runs through my mind and I shiver.

I turn away to catch up with Bron. He has already disappeared into the maze of pathways through the woods, but I can always find him. A young boy and his imaginary friend are nothing if not inseparable.

When I blink into existence by Bron's side he is panting heavily while pushing his way through the thick tangle of woods. He is lost, and if the fear in his eyes were any more tangible I could pluck it free with my own hand. Of course, I would have to be tangible as well.

He has fallen off the paths, gotten turned around, and is limping through the brush now.

[*Bron... just calm down, my friend.*]

He listens to me, stopping and leaning against a thick tree to catch his breath. I survey the area. There are flashes of movement through the trees all around. Yelling, garbled and indistinct, echoes back and forth through the woods. But nothing too close, yet.

[*You are in no immediate danger, they are probably still following the paths and looking for the Goodpaws.*]

He looks at me and says, "Teddy?"

[*Quiet!*]

At least he was out of breath enough that it came out barely above a whisper.

[*I have to get Teddy, he is just a kid.*]

[*YOU are just a kid, forget him. Forget them all, Bron. You HAVE to save yourself. These psychopaths are not playing around.*]

"No!"

He sounds angry. It dispels a touch of the fear from his eyes. That's good, but I need him to make the smart choices here, so I don't have to watch helplessly as he is pummelled to death. So I say nothing and just look at him.

Finally he makes a decision and begins to move back the way he came. I don't know if this is a good thing or not, as I am just as lost as Bron is. He manages to find a path through the woods and heads off towards Bruknows. I think he is heading in the right direction.

There is a burst of movement and sudden yelling from behind us and Bron breaks into a startled sprint. We can both hear them just behind us. The yelling gets louder, more excited, as the high schoolers close in on Bron. They are getting closer and closer, and Bron's eyes keep getting wider and wider as exhaustion and fear both threaten to overwhelm him.

He stumbles then, colliding with a tree in the path and spinning himself around and to the ground. He gets up quickly, but something has changed in his eyes. The fear is gone.

[*Bron?*]

I can hear the crashing of the high schoolers getting closer.

[Chaid?] He replies.

[*What are you doing? Run!*]

[No, I'm not going to run anymore.]

I was wrong, the fear is still there, but there is something else overshadowing it.

[*They are going to hurt you, Bron please!*]

[I'll be ok, Chaid, don't worry.]

I wonder for a fleeting moment if he has lost it, or if he took a hit to the head and dazed himself against that tree, but neither is true. I recognize the stubbornness in his eyes; and watch as it blazes into something new. He is angry. Not just angry, but outraged. And then he confirms it for me.

[I'll not be pushed around any longer.]

I nod and try to give him an encouraging smile. I am proud, frightened for his well being and continued existence, but still proud that he is finally standing up for himself.

[*I will stand next to you, my friend.*]

He smiles a weary smile back at me and nods. It's nice to see his eyes clear of the terror and shame that is usually carried around within them. They are set... determined.

The crashing gets louder and a couple of the hockey stick wielding high schoolers rush down the path towards Bron. They only glance at Bron before rushing past and continuing down the path.

I can't believe it.

Bron doesn't move, just keeps standing there. Whether he is stunned or just too exhausted to react, I don't know. He probably just can't believe it either. They left him alone.

Another couple of high schoolers appear on the path. Bron stands his ground again. The first one runs past and I can see the beginnings of a smile tug at the edges of Bron's lips. Then the second kid lurches to a stop and looks at Bron in disbelief.

I feel a mountain sized rock sink into the pit of my stomach and I feel like I am going to be sick. Bron's hint of a smile is shocked out of existence and he goes very, very pale. He looks like he also wants to be sick. He stands there very still, very quiet, very much waiting for the very worst to begin. What he doesn't do, however, is run.

"Look at this dumb-ass, just standing here pretending he isn't going to get the beating of his life!"

The first kid returns, chuckling, and three others appear on the path and now Bron is surrounded by five of them. The one who recognized Bron is holding a bat and raises it slowly to just under Bron's chin. He grins, the others keep chuckling darkly, and he tilts Bron's chin back with a gentle push of the bat.

"Did you think you were going to get away with it, dumb-ass? You think we're stupid or something? You think you're not going to get the same as your friends?"

Bron doesn't answer, he doesn't make a sound, and his eyes remain dry. He stands his ground, chin now tilted almost painfully back. His usual cool blue eyes are darker, like the sky at the edge of a storm. They glare defiantly back at the high schooler.

"Come on, dumb-ass, aren't you going to beg? You got a death wish or something? Come on, give us a few tears and maybe we'll let you limp out of here... Come on... BEG!"

The kid is shouting into Bron's face now, and if he pushes Bron's chin any farther back Bron is going to fall backwards. Bron is not backing down though.

I step up behind Bron and let my hands rest on his shoulders. I do this for support, but I can also feel what is flowing through him. It's like a current of sensation that I'm tapped into. He is still scared. He is still so sick and tired of being scared. He is still angry at them, at himself, at everyone and anyone who ever made him feel scared. He is still determined not to be a victim of anyone or anything anymore. He still believes he is doing the right thing, the brave thing, and that he is going to walk out of here unharmed.

[*Bron, you do not have to do this. There are five of them. They are all bigger than you and they are armed. It is not cowardly to recognize when you cannot win.*]

The baseball bat wielding kid leans in close, still holding Bron's chin way back. He says quietly, "all you have to do is beg, kid." He is almost whispering, with a big grin on his face as he continues tormenting Bron. "Beg us to leave you alone and we'll let you go."

He was always stubborn, like a small rod of steel buried within him, but right now that inner core of metal is white hot. Beyond anything else, right now Bron is very, very angry.

He tilts his head forward, shaking as he struggles against the pressure of the bat. Bron pushes back until his head is straight once more, held high and staring back at the high schooler.

The kid is reaching his second hand for the bat. His grin twists into a grimace and he opens his mouth to say something. He looks like he is going to start yelling again. Bron beats him to the punch.

"NO!"

They flinch. One of them even takes a step back. Bron is loud, not screaming but yelling in a deep toned voice I have never heard before.

"You want me to beg? Beg you? I'd rather die, you pathetic, worthless, inbred, hick, morons! You think I don't know who you all are?"

Bron's eyes travel around, landing on each of

them in turn, "Mark... Ryan... Greg... Brad... Chris! Beg you? You beg me!"

Bron is on a roll and I am loving it. "Beg me not to tell your parents, beg me not to tell the cops, beg me not to tell everyone in the world that you had to gang up five to one, armed with bats and hockey sticks, to beat up one little kid four years younger than you! Beg me not to tell them that this... THIS is what you have to do to feel like you're worth ANYTHING!"

The bat falls away from Bron's chin, the look on Mark's face is priceless. Total disbelief. Shock. A touch of fear. Maybe a bit more than just a touch.

"Go on... YOU BEG ME..."

The bat connects to the side of Bron's face with a crack that sounds like a gunshot going off. It cuts Bron off instantly and he collapses to his hands and knees. I am still standing there with my hands outstretched, though they now rest on empty air. I feel nothing.

Bron looks up. His face bloodied, his ear bashed with blood pouring from it, his left eye already beginning to swell closed. Blood is leaking from his nose as well. It's a miracle he is still conscious, that he can remain on his hands and knees.

He looks at Mark, his one open eye still blazing with righteous indignation. Still not backing down, he starts to rise back to his feet and manages to choke out a quiet, "go... to hell... you worthless..."

All five of them fall on him, encircling him with their sticks rising and falling and beating Bron down into the dirt. He goes down. He doesn't get back up. After a few minutes they leave without saying anything. Bron lies in the dirt, unmoving.

>I stand over his body.
>I do nothing.
>I am helpless.

❖ 3 ❖

Three weeks. Bron still lives, if the endless stillness he is trapped in could be called living. They call it a coma, the doctors. They test and consult results and shake their heads and say that it is up to Bron now. I listen to them as they whisper to the nurses. No one talks very loud in Bron's room, as if they are afraid he will overhear.

I still talk to him, though I don't know what to say. I would like to tell him that his classmates come by to visit. That they come by and wish him well and pray he wakes soon. I would tell him of the pretty girl he always did like. That she visits, weeps and is ever so sorry she had ignored him. I would tell him how the Castors, his foster folks, had come by to comfort their darling foster boy. I would love, above all, to tell him how everyone had come by to say how sorry they were. How they would always regret not being able to make it up to him - if he didn't wake up. I would like to, but I do not. I don't lie to Bron, not if I can help it.

I am leaning against the wall in the hallway just outside of his room. It is late and the place is quiet. Too still and calm. Too... accepting. I want to scream and yell at the orderly calmly eating his night shift "lunch" just down the hallway. I want to reach out and grab the doctor coming around the corner to start her rounds. I want to toss her through a wall. I want them to do more. They should be doing something more, anything more to help Bron. I want my friend back.

[Chaid?]

I am by his side in less than the blink of an eye, before he has even finished saying my name. I am there, and he looks up at me through gummy eyes and tries to smile around the tubes secured to his face.

[*Bron, my friend, how you gave me a scare!*]

[Sorry Chaid, didn't mean to.]

[*I know, do not worry yourself overmuch about it. I am just glad to see you awake. Are you ok?*]

He tries to nod his head, which pulls on something that is still attached uncomfortably to his body. He grimaces, but whether in pain or just annoyance I don't know.

[How long was I out, Chaid?]

[*Not all that long. Bron, you should rest until the doctors come get you cleaned up. I would not want you to pull something lose or hurt yourself.*]

[You don't think I have rested long enough then?]

His hand moves, slightly. He is looking at it and I can tell it is taking a lot for him to move it. I worry, but am still glad to see his fingers twitch. I smile and catch it reflected in his eyes as he glances at me before looking down towards his feet. A few minutes later he manages to wiggle his toes.

[*Well done my friend.*]

He nods and smiles just enough for me to see and then, using his eyes only, glances around his little room. His gaze wanders over to rest upon a nearby chair. It is empty. It has been empty the entire time Bron has been here.

[Chaid...]

He trails off. He doesn't ask me the questions I know are burning in his mind. I may not lie to my friend, but that doesn't mean I have to reveal every truth to him. So I say nothing.

His eyes wander once more. This time they wander over to rest upon me. Within them I can see a smoldering ember remaining of the courage it took for him to stand up for himself that day three weeks ago. It is there, but it is weak.

[Chaid?]

I still do not answer him, but cannot bring myself to look away. I so very desperately do not want to see that ember snuffed out completely.

Bron looks away, his eyes glimmering as he fights back tears. He manages not to cry.

[It's ok, Chaid. I am glad you are here. I think... I think I will try to sleep. I am tired.]

[*That is good, my friend.*]

[You will still be here when I wake up, right Chaid?]

[*Of that, you can always be sure of.*]

Bron closes his eyes. I do not know if he actually goes to sleep or is just pretending, but I leave him be. It is an extraordinary amount of pain for a young boy to deal with, but I would have him do so with dignity instead of wallowing in pity. Mine, his own, or anyone else's.

❖ 4 ❖

Bron sleeps, uncomfortably so it would seem since he keeps shifting around in the sleeping bag. I wonder if he is having a nightmare. The ground is not the most comfortable looking, but the sleeping bag is a pretty good one. It was one of the things I made him wait for, along with a whole list of other decent supplies.

He, and I really can't blame him for this, wanted to leave the day he got out of the hospital. However, he did agree with me that the only thing worse than staying in Shaw would be to run away only to get caught and drug back. So we waited patiently, planned, and prepared.

A low moan escapes Bron and I look over at him, concerned.

"Chaid?"

He is speaking to me out loud, but we are alone so that is ok. He rolls over, eyes wide and clear of sleep. I can see a flicker of reflected firelight in his troubled eyes.

[*Bad dreams again?*]

He blinks, looks up at me and then glances back towards Shaw. It is three days distant now, but that doesn't mean much when you can see forever across the flat prairies. He keeps staring and I join him.

The night is clear overhead, but behind us there are clouds. Under-lit by the town's streetlights, they churn over Shaw. A summer storm, perhaps.

I turn back to find Bron once more staring at me silently. I say nothing, letting him get on with it in his own time.

"Bad dream," he says quietly, "the same one over and over again. Actually, I have been having it for months now."

[*You want to tell me about it?*]

He nods. "Yes, but... I don't think I will have it again. It felt different this time... final..."

I do not really know what he means by this. So I wait for him to start and after a moment to gather his thoughts, he does.

"It starts the same, even though other parts of the dream are sometimes different.

I am standing, barefoot in the wasteland. I should be worried about hurting my feet, but the ground is not rocky or sandy. It is soft, like some kind of hard packed powder. It stretches on forever, the same grey nothing in all directions. It looks empty, but I know that it isn't. I can feel something out there, something hungry. It is very frightening, the nothing that is not empty... the nothing that is very hungry.

Anyway, a wind gusts suddenly, blowing powder around and blinding me. I taste it on my lips, bitter and gross. Then it is all gone and I am standing somewhere in Shaw. Or so it would seem, but when I look down I can still see my bare feet on the hard packed ash of the wasteland.

The town is on fire. Sometimes it is just starting, sometimes I dream that it is already completely in flames. I am not afraid of being burned, but can feel that hunger grow stronger out in the nothing wasteland.

The fire spreads quickly through the town. Too quickly. No one escapes. Everyone in the town dies.

Their screams begin suddenly, all at once and do not die out quickly. I listen to every one of them burn slowly to death.

Whatever is out there in the wasteland starts to fade away. It is fed, full now, and slipping into slumber. The last of the burning screams also fade as Shaw is reduced to ash..."

Bron fades off, but I say nothing. I know he is not quite finished and it is this last part that is most difficult for him.

He is staring into the fire. Mesmerized.

"I felt it, Chaid. Over and over again, the same dream. Listening and watching all of them die so horribly. It was so real and..."

He finally looks up at me and in his eyes I can see that same resolve. That courage and dignity forged behind Bruknows hill. It is lacking something though. Some essential spark that no longer flickers within.

I can hear its absence in his voice, flat and distant, as he continues, "...and I didn't care."

A little boy, with all sense of hope destroyed.

"I know I should care, but I don't feel anything for them, good or bad... just... nothing..."

I say nothing, but I nod. Bron stares at me a moment, then silently rolls over to go back to sleep. I wonder if it is even possible for me to bring hope back to this child. I do not know.

I glance back towards Shaw. Hope may or may not be within my power, but I have found that I am far from helpless. The clouds above the town keep getting thicker. The reflected light from the town keeps getting brighter. The light is red and flickering. The clouds are smoke. It is too far away to hear the screams, but I can imagine them. The whole town will be dead by morning.

I find that I, too, do not care.

- Chapter 2: Joy -

"Joy is taking what is yours and making it mine. Bliss is seeing the look on your face when it hits you; the realization that you have lost." – *unknown*

❖ 1 ❖

"Firefighters struggled against the out of control inferno throughout the night and most of the following day. Experts are baffled as to how such a blaze could have spread so rapidly, leaving the small prairie town thoroughly decimated. Casualties are in the..."

I stop listening and, thankfully, Glen switches the channel away from the news. Then again, the latest rerun of the current sitcom sensation is even more boring and frustrating to listen to. The desire to tear my hair out continues to get stronger.

Absently, I pace some more. If he could see me -if I were a real live boy- I am sure Glen would have kicked me out of the house for wearing a path through his living room carpet by now.

I stop in front of the stairs that lead up to her room and can't help but go check, hoping she has returned. The room is empty. I sit there, in the silence of her absence, for as long as I can stand it.

Before my mind splinters in the silence, I leave the house and head into the nearby woods. Hidden within is the tree house where she and Nadia would sometimes hang out. They didn't build it, and it is not just their place, but it is a hideaway that adults don't know about. Nadia considered it safe, one of her favourite places. It sits empty, but at least it isn't silent.

I leave before the urge to scream at the cheerfully chirping chipmunks and birds overcomes me. I sit on a desk in a classroom, watching her favourite teacher mark projects. I visit the ice cream shop with the best hot fudge sundaes, already closed up for the day. I walk through the small town mall, ignoring the shoppers and only looking for her blazing red hair. I check a dozen other places she favoured. I wish I could find her, but she is still gone.

Finally I head to Nadia's house, but no one is home. At least, at first it feels like no one is home. Then, slithering down my back is the slimy feeling that someone is indeed in the house with me. Someone who shouldn't be here. Nadia's bedroom door is closed and from behind it I hear a soft, muffled whimper. I feel like I am eavesdropping on something I shouldn't know about, something I definitely do not want to know about. I don't want to be here any longer, but I make myself peek to make sure it's not her.

It isn't her, thankfully. But now I can't take back what I have seen. And I don't have anyone to tell about it.

Wandering almost aimlessly, feeling sick, lost, and useless, eventually I make it back home. Glen is still watching the same stupid sitcom. Not knowing how much longer I can take it, I finally give in and try to go directly to her. It is something that has always worked before, until now. I don't know how many more times I can try and fail before I truly lose my mind, but I can't stop. I can't give up.

I set my mind to thinking only about her. Her blazing red hair, all done up in that ridiculously cute peacock style that she still insists will catch on and make her famous. Her narrow face, pale and dotted with freckles. Her crooked grin, full of mischief, and those bright green eyes, sparkling with glee.

I concentrate.

[*Mab?*]

I blink.

[*MAB!*]

I blink again.

Nothing happens.

For as long as I can remember I have been Mab's closest friend. Sometimes I have been her only friend. Sure, I might be an imaginary friend, but that doesn't make our bond any less real. I have always been able to blink and appear right by her side, without really even needing to think about it. Just... blink... and I am right there with her.

Since she disappeared three weeks ago I have been alone. I can't blink to her side. I can't call out to her. I can't find her. She is just... gone.

[*Mab? Where are you?*]

I wish I could cry.

❖ 2 ❖

The whole mess started a couple of months ago. Mab woke up in the middle of the night, crying. Not screaming or yelling, just crying about a nightmare. I was there, of course, right by her side...

[*Mab, are you alright, my dear?*]

She doesn't look up, face hidden beneath a tangled mess of hair.

[*Mab?*]

[Yes, Chaid. I'm fine, just... give me a minute will ya?]

I nod silently, which is stupid since she isn't even looking at me. But my silence will be enough of an answer for her and I even step back a bit to let her have her space.

What kind of imaginary friend would I be if I wasn't supportive?

While I think about this, I fall right out of the tree house. Yelling, more in surprise than fright, I hit the ground.

"Chaid!," she yells in concern.

Muttering, [*stupid... railing-less... bug infested... dirty... stick and spit death trap,*] I pick myself up off the ground.

She laughs, and I can't help but lift my head to grin back at her. It's not the most enchanting sound, her laugh, but it is always music to my ears.

At the edge of the tree house platform she peers down at me. Face shrouded in darkness, backlit by the half moon above. I can still make out the wide grin on her face.

[Silly Chaid... always gotta be the centre of attention.]

[*Oh yes, silly me.*] I bow with a flourish. [*Well, if breaking my neck is what is required to entertain you, I do believe it is time to give it up altogether.*]

She laughs even more, losing all control and

just letting her mirth take over. She does that a lot.

[What else can you do other than be a fool for me?]

[*Oh vexing vixen, how you do wound me with your scathing words. Adding insult to my injury...*]

[Chaid, you can't even be hurt, stupid!]

[*Yeah, yeah, yeah...*]

[Chaid,] she cuts me off again, but this time it is the sudden lack of laughing cheer in her voice that gives me pause, [how come we're in the tree house?]

...and she was right, it had been a school night and she had gone to bed at home. At first we worried that she had been sleepwalking, but her feet were clean. She gave the idea of a possible kidnapper all of five seconds of consideration before laughing that one away. It worried her for a few short minutes before her natural carefree mind reasserted itself. She just shrugged it off as a mystery not really worth too much of her consideration, and we went home.

Three days later, in another of a long line of attempts to out prank her, a school friend set a locker trap that startled Mab quite successfully and... blink... we were both at the tree house again. Thankfully no one was in the hall at the time to see her disappear.

It should have been concerning, frightening, or even terrifying. Instead, it was just a new amusing game. She explored the strange ability without fear or hesitation. A quality in her that I have always found endearing. Although I should have found this more than just a bit reckless, I could not help but admire her the more for it.

She seemed to master her new gift within weeks. Blinking here and there at will, with me in tow, and laughing all the while.

Then, three weeks ago, she just disappeared. Gone I don't know where, and I cannot get to her or find her.

❖ 3 ❖

Glen is watching another rerun episode of that stupid sitcom. The whole show is so simple, cliche, and stereotypical-driven crap that watching it is like sticking your brain in ice water. Numbing. Which may very well be why Glen is watching so much of it. Keeps him from going crazy worrying about Mab. She may not be his biological daughter, but he cares for her.

I catch myself absently chuckling at some of the absurd jokes on the sitcom and stop myself immediately. Shaking my head in disgust, I close my eyes and try to filter out the voices from the idiot box.

... blink...

It works, the voices are gone.

When she giggles, my eyes snap open and I am staring in disbelief. I'm at the tree house, and she is sitting there right in front of me with a big grin on her face. Her wondrous, freckled, and somewhat tanned face.

Where has she been?

[*MAB! My dear, where have you been?*]

She, laughing even more in her infectious merriment, tackle hugs me.

"Oh Chaid, I missed you!"

Which does not answer my question.

She sits back and smiles at me with all her charm. I wish I could say it fails to work, but she has always held me fully under her spell and I grin back at her.

A lock of her hair falls over her face and she shakes it away. A light dusting of some kind of pale grey grit falls from her. I look closer and realize she is covered in it. It looks like ash.

"It was amazing Chaid, I blinked all over the place. I wanted to see how far I could go, how fast, and how often before I would get tired. I saw great cities, snowy mountain ranges as far as I could see, and deep canyons carved out of deserts... all in one day!"

[*But,*] and it hurts me to have to ask this, [*why did you feel the need to go without me?*]

She pouts, and it takes a lot for me to not forgive her on the spot.

"Sorry, Chaid. I wanted to bring you, but I needed to test the limits of this… ability, and I didn't know if taking you with me would cause any problems."

It's a flimsy excuse, but she is smiling at me again and I feel forgiveness well on its way.

"I will take you with me next time, Chaid, promise."

[*I shall hold you to that promise, my dear. Now, you must tell me everything.*]

And she does. She tells me how she travelled all over and ended up on a tropical island. She stayed there for most of the three weeks, exploring the island and learning to surf. She leaves out the bit about the boy she met, but I read between the lines of her story.

[*Why come home now?*]

I ask, wondering if she and the boy had gotten into a fight or something. Wondering if she would tell me about him. Dreading it.

Instead, her almost always joyous face pales and she looks... scared.

"I started to notice people staring at me. Like, really staring. They would just stop in the middle of whatever they were doing, their whole face going all droopy like they were going to sleep. Then they would open their eyes and stare at me. It would last a minute or two, just staring without blinking."

[*The same people each time?*]

I am not going to question whether she is mistaken about what she had seen. Mab is mischievous, but very observant, and she has never lied to me or made up wild stories.

She shakes her head in response to my question. "No, sometimes they were strangers," she takes a deep breath, "and sometimes they were people I had met and knew... a little."

I avoid asking her about the boy, it becoming obvious that he had been one of the starers that had frightened her. Instead I sit and think, quietly, about what it can possibly mean.

Questions flood my mind. Was it some kind of supernatural possession? Was it some conspiracy or group of spying crazies? Was it a coincidence that it happened just after she discovered her abilities? I do not believe in coincidence.

Who or whatever was watching her did

nothing but watch, yet that does not reassure me that it meant her no harm. Instead it just creeps me out all the more.

I look up and find her sitting there watching me with a bit of a smile on her face, and it makes me smile to know that I can make her feel safe.

[*We shall figure it out, together, my dear. And now that you have returned, I shall ever be watchful for these... starers.*]

"Thanks, Chaid."

[*Think nothing of it, my dear.*]

"So, tell me what's been happening since I've been gone?"

I roll my eyes, [*like anything interesting could happen without you here!*]

She snorts, most un-lady-like, and shoves me playfully. "No really, how much trouble am I in, and how is Glen?"

[*No small amount of trouble, I should think. It has been three weeks, my dear. As for Glen,*] it's my turn to snort, [*watching all manner of mind numbingly horrible television. I truly dislike sitcoms.*]

She chuckles. "Why? They are not that bad, silly."

I throw my hands up in mock outrage.

[*They are just so stupid. Stupid jokes, stupid situations that make no sense, stupid people, stupid dialogue, stupid stereotypes, just... stupid. And yet, if you are not really paying attention to what you are doing, you find yourself laughing anyway.*]

My rant trails off at the end, because she is rolling around on the floor of the tree house, laughing her guts out. I wait for her to laugh it all out of her system, a look of stern upset fixed upon my face.

I notice that, in her rolling around, she has shaken most of the ash off of herself. Smears of it spread across the floorboards of the tree house. It is definitely ash.

"Oh Chaid..."

She is wiping tears from her face, that grin still there and she almost starts laughing again.

[*What?*]

"You're such a snob!"

I scowl, [*yeah, yeah, yeah.*]

She calms down and I sigh, because it is time for some seriousness. As much seriousness as she can handle. Maybe more.

[*Truly, Glen is worried sick about you, but that is not the worst thing.*]

Her smile fades and she listens attentively as I tell her about what I saw at Nadia's home. She is angry, very angry, but keeps herself from launching into a useless rant.

A short time later she has a plan. It is both daring and reckless. It will, if it works, deal with both Nadia and the problem of explaining Mab's disappearance. I like it.

We stay up most of the night, working out the details before she goes to sleep. But before I can let her drift off, I have to ask.

[*Mab?*]

[Yeah?]

She is really tired, not even realizing she isn't speaking out loud any longer.

[*How come you are covered in ash?*]

She starts to shrug, but is interrupted by a massive yawn.

[I don't know. Sometimes, when I am blinking a really long distance it isn't instant.]

[*You mean you were somewhere else, in between blinking from one place to another?*]

She tries to shrug again and only manages to yawn some more.

[Naw, well maybe... I only catch a glimpse of it, but it is always the same.]

I wait for her to continue, and then realize she has fallen asleep.

I scowl, but barely put any real effort into it.

I am just so glad she is back.

❖ 4 ❖

[*So, what is the plan?*]

"Chaid..."

I cut her off with a harsh, [*shhhhhhh!*]

We both peak out into the woods to see if anyone is nearby. On a weekday, around noon-ish, the chance of anyone being anywhere near the treehouse is slim.

[*There is no reason to push our luck, my dear, please.*]

My tone is polite, or at least I try to make it so. She still rolls her eyes and gives me a glare. As if I were some arrogant and ignorant adult making an unreasonable demand of her. I sigh, but she does go on without speaking out loud.

[Fine. What I was gonna say is that we have

gone over it already, Chaid. So let's just get on with it already!]

[*Indulge me then.*]

Another glare, this one heated. I am glad that looks cannot kill, though I wonder if that rule still holds true when one is merely a figment of the glarer's imagination.

[Ugh, fine! First we need to make sure Nadia is safe. I'll need you to do some scouting so I can nab her on the way home from school without her...]

She pauses to shudder.

[... father catching us.]

I nod, but then something crosses my mind. She must see it on my face, because she stops and raises one eyebrow in curiosity.

[*I did not think to ask before, my dear, but how do you know you can take someone else with you when you blink?*]

She looks down a second before answering. I think she is blushing.

[I've done it before, on the island.]

Her boy. I question her no further on the matter and hope that my face does not betray that I am upset. I motion, a quick twirl of my finger, for her to continue.

[Right, so I nab her and bring her somewhere safe and out of the way.]

[*You still do not think she would help us?*]

Mab looks uncomfortable, or just a bit lost. She is, after all, only in grade seven and this is an awful lot for someone so young to handle. I am proud to see that, while she struggles with it all, she is in no way backing down.

[I don't know. Maybe she would, but maybe she would be too scared.]

I place a hand on her shoulder and smile warmly. [*You are a good friend, my dear. Nadia is lucky to have someone like you to save her.*]

She nods and smiles back. [Then we wait. You keep an eye on the place and when the time is right we spring the trap on him. He goes to prison for life, I have an excuse for being missing, and Nadia is safe. You think she could come live with us?]

[*We can only hope, my dear. Regardless, she will be safer, thanks to you.*]

With a big smile on her face, she nods enthusiastically and jumps up.

"Let's get started!"

I stand up with her and the joy on her face is such that I cannot even scold her for yelling out loud. She takes my hand and we... blink...

When I open my eyes we are standing in a snowbank. The snow around us is unbroken by footprints. A brisk wind blows loose snow into a brief whirlwind around us. Mab shivers, but there is a grin on her face. Probably one on my face too. The view of the rocky blue-grey and white capped mountains all around us is spectacular.

We turn and she points out the cabin. We head towards it to prepare.

Only one set of footprints through the snow is left behind.

❖ 5 ❖

Nadia has been following roughly the same schedule every day so far this week. The final bell goes and the school explodes with kids rushing to get away. The school yard clears, mostly, and Nadia finally leaves the school. She walks alone, and always follows the same path through a kiddie park near the woods and then home. With no reason to believe she will deviate from this schedule, I think it is time to put step one of the plan into action.

I watch for a few more minutes as the last school buses head out of the school yard. A few straggling kids are playing in the yard, but none of them will see me. I follow Nadia as she heads directly towards the park.

I think of her and... blink... I am by Mab's side in the mountain cabin. She jumps up, an eager smile on her face.

[*My dear, it is time.*]

She claps and then grasps my hand and we... blink... and now we are crouched in the bushes at the edge of the kiddie park. It is empty.

So far, so good.

Right on cue, Nadia walks through the gap in the chain link fence and enters the park. She is alone. I had not thought of it before, but Mab must be the girl's only friend. I glance to my side to peer at Mab, who is wearing an eager smile of anticipation. If Nadia only knew what an amazing friend she had. Then I smile, because she is about to find out.

As Nadia passes close by, Mab sneaks out, keeping low as she slinks up behind her unsuspecting friend. I keep close.

"Nadia," she whispers and clasps Nadia's hand from behind. I grab Mab's hand at the same time and before Nadia can react we, all three of us... blink...

Except when I open my eyes we are not at the cabin. Mab's hand is still firmly gripped in my own, but I cannot see her or Nadia. There is nothing but a howling whirlwind of ash grey grit swirling around me.

I cannot see or feel anything. Except, that is not entirely true, I do suddenly feel something. It is a hunger, awakening from deep within me. A hunger I have never felt before. It is immediate and overwhelming, and though I relish the strange new sensation, it feels like a hunger I could never satisfy.

[*What. In. All. Creation?*]

Very faintly I hear a little girl scream from nearby, but the shrill sound is mostly lost to the roar of the whirlwind storm.

It lasts all of a couple of seconds, or an eternity, then it is gone.

We all collapse to the floor of the cabin.

❖ 6 ❖

The first to recover is Nadia and, to her credit, she doesn't scream. She pulls herself into a sitting position on the heavy rug and looks around the room. A thin layer of dull grey ash covers her, darkening into tear stained streaks beneath her very wide eyes.

With a shake to clear the grit from her face, she pulls herself over to Mab and shakes her. Mab doesn't move. I find I cannot move either.

An hour later I start regaining the ability to move, but oh so very slowly. During that hour of immobility I watch Nadia explore the rustic log cabin, cry for a while, go outside into the wintery cold and immediately return, drag a blanket over to make Mab comfortable, and cry a little more. As soon as I can, I make it over to Mab and am overjoyed to find her eyes shift to meet mine.

The plan changes, has to change, considering Nadia has to take care of Mab while she regains her strength over the next three days.

"Thank you, Nadia," Mab says as her friend spoons hot chicken noodle soup for her to eat.

Nadia nods, looks around at the log cabin again, as if still unsure it truly exists, then turns back to Mab.

"You gonna tell me what's going on now?"

Nadia's voice is quiet, one might say meek, but I now think otherwise. She is a girl who has learned to carefully hide every part of herself away.

Mab nods.

[*You think she will help us now, my dear?*]

Mab continues to nod, but stays focussed on Nadia.

"I can... travel... anywhere I want in just a blink. Been learning how to use it for the past few months."

Nadia thinks about this for a moment, spooning another mouthful of soup into Mab's mouth.

"That's how we got here," she says, more of a statement to be accepted than a question. Then she does ask Mab a question, "why me?"

Mab smiles, that wondrously foolish smile of

hers. "Cause you're my friend, stupid, and," her smile fades, "I had to save you."

The spoon, full of another mouthful of soup, pauses on its way to Mab's mouth. Nadia's quiet voice quiets further, as she nearly whispers, "save me from what?"

Mab's smile is now gone. "Your dad."

The spoon drops into the now trembling bowl. "My dad," Nadia looks into Mab's eyes as she places the shaking bowl of soup onto the table, "what do you know about my dad?"

"I know he hurts you."

Mab looks like she is going to say more, but Nadia interrupts her by asking, "how?"

"I just do, I..." Mab starts to reply.

"I NEED TO KNOW!"

Nadia doesn't have to be quiet if she doesn't want to. The whole cabin has been shocked into silence by Nadia's outburst. I notice that she has stopped shaking, but I do not know if this is a good thing or a bad thing.

[I'm going to tell her, Chaid.]

"I have another friend, Nadia. He is special too," starts Mab.

[*What? Mab, no!*]

"Special how?"

[I have to.]

"Well, he can go anywhere he wants, cause no one can see or hear him. No one but me."

I can't believe what I am hearing. [*This, my dear, is a colossal mistake.*]

"When I was gone for those three weeks he was

looking for me. He went looking for me at your home. When I got back a few days ago, he told me about your dad."

[*Mab!*]

Mab shoots me a glare, "shhhhhh!"

Nadia looks up and glances in my direction. The direction Mab is glaring in. There are tears trickling down her cheeks. She absently wipes them away with her shirt sleeve as she peers at the empty space I occupy.

"He is here, with us, right now?"

Mab nods, a bit of a smile on her face again, "yep."

Mab then points to the window on the opposite side of the cabin from her.

"Go over to the window and say something in a whisper, something I couldn't possibly hear. Chaid will listen and then tell me."

[*Or perhaps I will do no such thing.*]

Nadia nods, but only faintly.

[Chaid, she needs to believe me.]

But she is making no effort to get up to go over to the other side of the cabin.

[*Does she now, and just why would that be so important?*]

She is watching Mab though, as Mab's face reddens in anger.

[Because I need her to, come on Chaid.]

Mab's face is getting redder, but the anger is shifting quickly to embarrassment.

[*Just what exactly is it that you need?*]

I don't know what my face looks like.

[I need...] she stammers.
[*Yes?*]
[I...]

But I know that I am very angry. I am almost shouting at her, [*WHAT?*]

"Chaid," Nadia says quietly and I turn immediately to watch her rise from the table and walk over to the other side of the cabin, "come listen."

I glance back at Mab, who is no longer angry or embarrassed, but looks ready to cry. I am suddenly ashamed of myself. I wish it made my anger diminish, but it does not.

I stalk silently over to stand next to Nadia. She whispers and I listen. I walk over to Mab and repeat it, then I sit over in the corner by myself.

Mab is calming down as Nadia returns to the table.

"So, what did I whisper?" She asks Mab.

Mab smiles a not-so-cheerful smile as she replies, "he told me that you said you love the mountains, but wished we had a horse so we could go riding through the snow."

Nadia smiles and nods, but I can see that she does not quite believe just yet. I do not know if Mab sees this as well. I refuse to look at Mab right now.

"He also told me that he thinks you're cute, but I wasn't supposed to tell you that." Mab adds in with a short giggle.

I shoot a glare off at Mab, but she just shoots a smile back at me. I should be more angry. I want to be more angry, but find that I am already cooling off.

Nadia also giggles, but like Mab, it only lasts a

short moment. She picks up the bowl of cooling soup, but Mab shakes her head.

"I am good, thanks. I feel much better."

Then, either to emphasize her point or because she does indeed see that Nadia still does not fully believe, Mab winks at her and... blinks...

She just disappears. One moment she is there, sitting at the table all wrapped up in a blanket, then the chair is empty and Mab is gone.

I sigh. Nadia just stares, wide eyed. Before either of us can react in any other way, we both hear Mab's giggle from the other side of the cabin, where she is curled up in her blanket on the rickety old bed.

[*You are definitely feeling more like yourself.*] I say, mostly to myself since I am still too angry to be speaking to her.

Cheerfully she replies, "yup, I am!"

Nadia stares for a minute, then picks up the spoon and quietly finishes the last of the chicken noodle soup.

❖ 7 ❖

We decide that Mab and Nadia will blink back home without me. Perhaps taking both me and Nadia so long a distance was what was so overwhelming to her, and I can always blink to Mab's side on my own. Well, usually I can, when she wants me around. I am still a little upset that she can and has blocked me. Standing around the empty log cabin for a minute or so, not knowing if Mab is ok or not, does not help my mood.

Finally I... blink... and appear next to Mab and Nadia in the tree house. They both appear fine, Mab with a big grin on her face as she sees me appear.

Mab reaches out and takes Nadia's hand and they... blink... away. The plan is to deposit Nadia in the woods just outside the closest neighbouring town, where she can go tell her story to the local cops.

Mab is back in only a few minutes, but her coat and boots are gone. She pulls off her socks and messes up her hair.

[*Are you sure about this?*]

She nods. "Of course. I know the room Nadia told us about, in the basement. Go scout it out."

I nod and start to leave.

[Chaid.]

I stop.

[Thank you.]

I nod again, then go.

Nadia's father is home. Not surprising, considering his daughter is the second little girl kidnapped from this community in the past month.

He is sitting in the living room, a mostly empty bottle of vodka in his hand, watching sitcoms. I snort.

[*Pathetic wretch of a man.*]

I scout out the room as well, since Mab isn't going to have a lot of time to move around the house with Nadia's father home. It is just as Nadia described it, a small basement room of featureless concrete. Nothing in it but a leaky water heater and a gun cabinet. The outside of the door has a padlock on it though, again like Nadia said. Perfect.

I go to Mab's side and give my report and we both... blink... directly into the room. Mab goes over the entire place, touching everything, making sure it seems like she has been there for a while. I keep an eye on Nadia's father in case he manages to rouse himself from the couch. While I am keeping watch Mab just sits in the room looking cold and miserable while we wait.

We don't have to wait too long. The police arrive after about an hour. They find Mab, the poor missing little girl locked away in a monster's basement room, to the utter disbelief of Nadia's father. He is arrested, Mab is rescued, the case of the town's two missing children is solved, and before the night is over Mab is being crushed in one of Glen's famous bear hugs.

Mab is happy to see Glen, and even I have to admit it is good to see him focussed and happy instead of zoned out in front of one of those ridiculous sitcoms.

❖ 8 ❖

Later that night Mab is lying in bed at the hospital. The doctors say she appears to be fine, but will be here for a little while for observation. Glen is snoring in a chair nearby. Nothing they said would drive him away from her side. Mab, of course, is perfectly fine. More than fine, she is giddy with excitement.

[Chaid...]

I am right there by her side.

[*Yes, my dear?*]

She muffles a giggle in a bunched up blanket.

[It worked!]

[*Yes, it did indeed. Well done.*]

[Can you do me a favour, please?]

[*And this favour you would ask of me, it would be*

what?]

She scowls a bit, realizing that there is still a small part of me that is mad at her. But she is asking nicely, instead of assuming I will just do whatever she is about to ask of me.

I know, of course, that I will indeed do whatever she asks, regardless. What I don't know is whether or not she knows this.

[I gotta see how Nadia is doing and make sure she isn't freaking out. Can you keep an eye on Glen. Let me know if he wakes up so I can blink back?]

She gives me a big smile, [please, please, please...]

[*Oh, very well. Just go then, but no more telling her lies about what I do or do not say.*]

She has to muffle another round of giggles in the blanket, but finally she nods and then... blinks... away.

I sit and watch Glen snore. It's boring, yet still much better than watching sitcoms.

❖ 9 ❖

Later, though I cannot be sure how much later, I hear a nurse beginning to make his or her rounds. Checking in on the patients in the very early and still very dark morning.

I glance over to the still snoring Glen and wonder how long I have before it is discovered that Mab is, once again, missing.

I... blink... and am instantly by her side.

"Chaid," she exclaims in surprise as I appear.

Nadia looks up, curled up in a blanket and

looking... well, just tired.

[*It is time to return, my dear. The nursing staff will be checking in on you and Glen may wake any moment now.*]

She nods, but reluctantly as she glances at Nadia and gives her a hug goodbye.

I take Mab's hand and after a moment of hesitation, we... blink...

We do not appear in the hospital.

The wasteland appears before us, again. Instead of a whirlwind, it is an endless landscape of grey ash. It blurs along an indistinct horizon line that finally shifts into a sky coloured the purplish shade of a fresh bruise. We are not standing in it this time, instead we crouch in a room high above it.

The building appears to be made out of the same ash as the wasteland. Hard packed and yet still soft beneath our feet. The room is otherwise featureless, having only a window-like opening before us and a spiraling set of stairs leading both up and down.

The window looks out over the wasteland. There is no sound. Nothing moves. Yet, I feel that hunger return, surging up from within me. It... it is... uncontainable... endless...

Lost as I am in the razored clutches of this need to consume... something, I still manage to realize that Mab has suddenly shrunk away from the window in fright.

I move forward to see what it is, still ever her protector, and stumble across the ash floor. A puff of grey dust rises up from my impact. Even through the hunger and concern for Mab, I am momentarily stunned by the revelation that I actually hit the floor. I rise and can see the imprint left in the ash by my body.

"Chaid?"

"I am," I whisper to myself, "I am real."

"Chaid!" she says again, this time much more insistent.

It's Mab, and the thick fear that I can sense in her draws me back to my concern for her safety. Yet the hunger still gnaws constantly at me. I struggle to crawl over to her, leaving a dragging set of hand and footprints behind me.

At the window I look out. Something is shuffling slowly across the wasteland near the base of the tower we are in. She, he, it... is bent over and haggard. Its body is lost in a shroud of black rags covered in layers of grey grit. I can hear the rasping of its uneven breathing from here, seeming to echo across the empty expanse of this place.

Cradled in its too long, too slender hands of grey flesh, is a bone white bowl. It is full of a thick, silvery liquid. It doesn't slosh around as the creature moves, so thick is the bowl's contents. As the creature pauses, the slow ripples of motion across the surface of the mercury-like fluid settles into a mirror to reflect the purple sky above.

It stops then and glances up. I think to myself, or perhaps wish or pray, that it cannot not see me. Amid the rags about its face I see a gleaming dark set of eyes. Everything goes quiet as they meet my own eyes, see me well, and pin me in place.

My excitement that, here, I am real. My strange and fearful hunger. Even my ever faithful concern for Mab's well being. All is lost to the terror that invades my soul through that thing's stare.

Darkness floods from those eyes, stabs into me and begins to shatter me into nothingness. The last thing I hear is Mab screaming. The last thing I see is that awful thing's leathery pale lips pull back into a hideous grin. The last thing I feel is a hunger that rivals my own, surge towards me with the hunter's glee of captured prey. And then I am lost.

❖ 10 ❖

I blink my eyes open and am met with a strange, unfamiliar room. Off white and very clean, separated into small sections by sheets hanging from the ceiling. A stranger lies in a strange bed and watches a tv on the wall. I cringe. A sitcom is playing. I fight the urge to both scream and giggle at the same time.

My mind grapples with what is going on, and I realize, eventually, that I am back in the hospital. I am in Mab's room, but she is no longer there. I have no sense of how long I have been gone.

Gone?

I remember everything, suddenly, hitting me like a sack of bricks. It takes some time for me to get a hold of myself. I am just about to blink directly to her side, but stop myself. I wonder, if I... if both Mab and I, are risking being caught by that thing every time we blink. I decide to walk to Glen's place instead.

"Chaid!"

Mab tackles me in a flying bear hug that takes

me off my feet and to the carpeted floor of her bedroom. Nadia sits on the bed, watching with an amused grin as Mab clings to an imaginary friend that doesn't appear to actually be there.

"I thought you were gone forever!"

She is crying and I am touched.

[*No, my dear. I do not believe anything has the power to truly keep me from you forever.*]

"What happened?"

[*Of that, I do not know. Only that I wish it to never happen again.*]

I comfort her until she is ready to release me. She cleans the tears from her freckled cheeks.

[*And are you well? That thing did not harm you did it?*]

She shakes her head. "It never saw me. You were gone a long time, Chaid, did it see you?"

[*Yes, it did, and when it did see me, something very bad happened and I was lost. For that, I do apologize, my dear Mab.*]

At this she laughs lightly and says, "tiss not your fault, stupid. It's that witch-thing that hurt you."

Witch-thing. I wish I could smile as I think how appropriate a description this is. She gives me a hug again, of which I am all too eager to give in to.

Nadia, in her careful quiet voice, cuts in, "I'm glad you're back, Chaid. It is scary when Mab disappears."

[*Disappears?*]

I fix Mab with a stern gaze. Well, what I hope is a stern gaze.

"I," she hesitates, but Nadia is also sending a

stern look Mab's way.

She sighs, then continues, "I went back to find you, when you were gone for so long. I thought maybe you were trapped in that awful place."

[*You were able to blink back to that place?*]

She nods.

"It took a couple of tries, but I made it. The witch thing was looking into that bowl."

My eyes must grow quite wide in alarm, because she quickly continues.

"It never saw me," she reassures me, but then gets quiet, "but it was watching Bron in that bowl."

[*WHAT?*]

"It was saying some kinda crazy words, words that made my head hurt. Then the silver stuff in the bowl faded and there was Bron's face in the bowl."

[*You are sure it was Bron? It has been a long time since last you did see him, my dear, and you were very young.*]

She nods, "It was him."

I nod, accepting it. If she thinks she saw Bron, then it was probably Bron. Even if it wasn't him, convincing her that she is wrong would be a long and futile battle that I have no interest in wasting time on losing.

I sit down and then stretch out on Mab's comfy bed. I am tired, very tired. Mab watches me for a minute and then turns to meet Nadia's glance. I know something else is up.

[*Yes, my dear? Out with it then.*]

Nadia and Mab hold each other's gaze a moment longer. Mab wears a saviour's grin on her mischievous face and although Nadia smiles back, I can see that the quiet girl is troubled.

"We're going to find Bron," Mab proclaims as she crosses her arms across her chest and nods, making any chance of a discussion or change of decision an impossibility, "find him and save him."

[*I guess that is...*] I struggle for a moment to find the right words, thinking about what kind of untapped power is still hidden within this crazy girl of mine, [*...possible.*]

- Chapter 3: A Girl -

"Power corrupts. Absolute power corrupts absolutely. What about the power to give it all up? Does this result in more or less power? Innocence or chaos? Freedom or subjugation?" – unknown

❖ 1 ❖

The school bus glides smoothly down the country lane, on its way back from a field trip. Of course, no one on the country lane seeing it will recognize it as a bus.

Built like a tank, the bus has a shell of thick armoured siding, painted matte black. Tinted windows hide slabs of bullet proof panelling. Emergency escape windows in the middle of each side of the bus are actually hidden intrusion countermeasures that draw in and take down assailants without anyone leaving the safety of the interior. The real emergency escape hatches are hidden in the floor and ceiling. The inside is sealed, pressurized, locked, guarded, and fully outfitted with every passenger safety feature currently on the market. I wouldn't be surprised to learn it has a couple features not yet on the market.

The Wiltshire-Ark community takes the safety of its children very... very... seriously. The only give away that this is a bus full of children, is the community's Academy logo on the side, near the forward door. I suddenly realize that not even this is going to give away the true nature of the vehicle, since no one is going to be on this road to see it. The lane and all the wilderness around it is owned and jealously guarded by the community.

Thinking about all this, as we continue down the road, I wonder how it should make me feel. If I wasn't a figment of a child's imagination, I believe it would make me feel very safe and, to only a slightly lesser degree, kind of paranoid. I try to hold on to that feeling though, for her sake.

"Hey, Miss Jordan... what are you always working on?"

The buzz of conversation around me quiets, snapping me out of my daydreaming, as several students look over at the teacher. She is sitting about halfway down the aisle, typing away rapidly on a personal tablet. She doesn't stop typing or answer the student's question.

Ashley's eyebrows rise in curiosity and more students quiet as they tune into what is going on, sharing Ashley's curiosity. Ashley is leaning out into the aisle a bit to get a clear look at Miss Jordan.

I shift a bit away from her seat to get out of the way. I don't know what would happen if she touched me, or if anyone touched me. They might feel something like a cold shock, or perhaps something even worse. Or maybe they would just pass through me like I was nothing but air. I don't know and I certainly have no desire to find out.

I catch a glimpse of Kendra, sitting beside Ashley, smirking at me suddenly.

[You're such an anti-social ghost, Chaid.]

I try to put as much cold disgust into my words as possible, [*I am... not... a ghost.*]

She giggles, quietly.

She and Ashley are very similar; both tall for their age, slim and very pretty. They both wear their hair just longer than shoulder length, but Ashley's pale blond and styled hair is always more eye-catching than Kendra's pale brown and plain hair. Ashley puts a lot of effort into being noticeable, while Kendra puts just as much effort, if not more, into blending into the background.

As the genuine smile spreads across her face and she forgets, for a moment, that she is supposed to be focussing on remaining unnoticed, Kendra changes. She relaxes, lets her guard fall, and reveals that she is more than just pretty. She is quite beautiful, stunning really.

It always catches me by surprise when it happens. It shouldn't, but she works so hard at keeping it hidden and she is very, very good at it.

"Kendra, you try. Miss Jordan likes you best."

And just like that, it is gone. Ashley turns back towards Kendra and before she can nudge Kendra with an elbow, the beauty fades and Kendra goes back to being plain again.

"Alright, alright. Move over so I can get out."

Ashley smiles, and Kendra slips by to move a couple of seats down the aisle, closer to the teacher who is still obliviously typing away at her tablet.

"Miss Jordan?"

Most of the kids who had quieted have already gone back to their chatter, but they quiet once more in interest as Miss Jordan's typing ceases.

"Yes, Kendra, what is it?"

"Um, just wondering if you're working on your

stand up comedy?"

The teacher chuckles. It isn't a fake or forced laugh in any way, but it cuts off suddenly as she fixes Kendra with a sudden and almost alarming stare of disappointment.

"No, no I am not."

Kendra almost starts to move away from the sudden appearance of anger on the teacher's face, but then grins and relaxes as she recognizes one of Miss Jordan's sarcastic gags.

"Oh, don't get me wrong, I wish I was, but you students are far too well behaved for me to get any real good material."

She huffs, putting on a show to the audience of grinning students on the bus who are all now paying attention.

"Really, at this rate it will be another five years before all of you give me enough material to retire and start my dream career as a stand up comedian."

Miss Jordan rolls her eyes over dramatically and Kendra struggles to stifle a giggle. A few of the other students chuckle.

"No, really. What are you working on, Miss Jordan? You're always writing whenever you get a chance. Is it a secret or something?"

The theatrics fade and the young teacher simply wears a warm smile as she turns towards Kendra.

"No, not a secret. I just don't like to make a big deal out of it. Don't wanna tempt fate and jinx it or anything."

She taps a couple of keys, and then hands the

tablet over to Kendra who carefully takes it and peers at the screen.

A big smile lights up Kendra's face, but even now she is aware of the other students still taking an interest. That other Kendra, the true Kendra who could take your breath away, stays hidden.

She hands the tablet back to the teacher, excitement written all over her face and in her voice, "you're writing a novel?"

Miss Jordan nods, her own smile growing as her excitement starts to reveal itself.

"Well, what's it about?"

Kendra starts in with the first question, but the rest of the students, Ashley included, quickly join in with their own questions.

"Can we read it?"

"Are we in it?"

"When will you finish it?"

"Is it about us?"

"Are you going to make any money from it?"

"Did you name one of the characters after me?"

And a barrage of, more or less, the same several questions continue until the bus is a racket of noise and no one can understand what anyone is saying anymore.

A loud, shrill whistle pierces the noise and puts everyone into sudden silence. A couple students, the ones sitting nearest the teacher, have clapped their hands over their ears. Miss Jordan knows how to get everyone's attention and silence.

Kendra has already slipped back to her seat next to Ashley, to avoid any more attention from the other students. Her interest is still held by Miss Jordan. I have to admit, even I am interested.

"Ok, ok. Shush up and I'll tell you."

Everyone is quiet, in rapt attention. Miss Jordan is great at many things, but her true talent is in telling amazing stories. Some of them are even somewhat true.

"It's about this young teacher who is just starting out in her teaching career. She has taken her first job, working for this big, mighty, and powerful private community academy."

She pauses a minute, with a not-so-slightly wicked grin on her face.

"She is teaching, oh... let's say a group of grade seven students."

Most of the students are wearing grins that mirror Miss Jordan's as they know her well enough to see where she is going with this story. Kendra is one of them and I wonder for a moment if Kendra would, if I could break her out of her shell, grow up to be as awesomely snarky as Miss Jordan.

"She loves her job, but oh," she pauses to quickly set an over dramatic look of troubled worry upon her face, "if only she didn't have to deal with such annoying and ungrateful students."

She chuckles, letting the wicked grin fall back into place, "so she finally gets fed up with them and makes them all disappear. And the rest of the novel is all about her wacky and zany adventures in trying to keep the disappearance of her entire class a secret so she can keep her job."

She sighs as she says, "it's a real tragedy."

The bus erupts in laughter. A big amused smile is on everyone in the bus. A few students start asking her more questions. Ashley and Kendra giggle, then huddle together and begin coming up with some elaborate plan to trick Miss Jordan into including them as characters in the novel. Miss Jordan is answering as many questions as she can and making promises to let everyone know when the novel is done so they can all get a copy.

I chuckle a bit myself. It sounds like one of Miss Jordan's overly-sarcastic stories and probably is not what the book is really about, but it's not a bad idea for a novel. I would read it. Well, I would want Kendra to read it so I could read it at the same time, peering over her shoulder.

I'm still chuckling, standing at the back of the bus when the explosion hits the side of the bus and shakes the world apart. A section of the bus wall crumples inward, everything flying into the air. Gravity disappears as the bus flips into the air and spins through space. Anything and anyone not buckled down or physically attached to something, is flung into a blender of chaos. I am sure everyone drawing breath is using it to scream at the top of their lungs, but the sound is lost to the roar and shriek of crumpling and tearing metal as the bus crashes to the ground and continues to tumble across the country lane.

I watch, unharmed and helpless. I can't even make out what is going on amid the chaos, but I still watch and wait for it to settle. I still exist, and I try to take some comfort from this. I would, no doubt, cease to be... if Kendra died.

The bus comes to a sudden and jarring halt, slamming everything to one side of the bus. The inside of the bus is silent for less than a second before it erupts in howls of terror and pain. The sound grows louder and louder and I stand there, willing the noise to keep getting louder. The more noise there is, the more kids there are who are still alive.

❖ 2 ❖

I can't find her, and although I should not be panicking, I am. I totally am. I can't find her, can't hear her, can't seem to find anyone even vaguely appearing to be her.

The bus has come to a rest on its side. Kids have been tossed all over the bus. Dozens of greenish-foam pillows have covered every inch of the inside of the bus -some sort of high tech, impact safety feature- and I can't recognize anyone in the mess.

Some of the students are trying to pick themselves up, some are stumbling aimlessly around, but most are just lying stunned or crying. Miss Jordan is being shaken by a couple of howling kids, but she is not responding. The section of the bus next to her has buckled inward, almost crushing her and a couple of the students. Hopefully she is only knocked out and not dead.

"Chaid?"

I look around wildly, not sure if I can believe my ears.

[Chaid... I can't move... help...]

I know I am not imagining that and I keep

looking around for her.

[*Kendra, I am here. Say something out loud again, so I can find you.*]

"Chaid! I'm over here... I'm... stuck!"

I find her, not far away of course. She is under a couple of school bags, covered in a pile of foam pillows and hopelessly tangled with an unconscious Ashley. She struggles to get free and get up, but keeps getting tangled.

[*Kendra, my dear. It is ok, I am here and you will be ok. Just slow down and you will get yourself free.*]

I reach out a hand and clasp hers, giving it a squeeze to let her know I am not going anywhere. She squeezes back and I catch a glimpse, through the tangle of straps and bags, of a strained smile from her.

A hand reaches past me from behind, almost touching me, and takes hold of her hand. I scramble to move out of the way and turn to see a bulky kid start to help pull her free. He is older than most of the kids on the bus, but not much taller. His blue eyes hold genuine concern within them, and for that I am glad.

"Easy now. I got you, just hold on."

He has a friendly voice. Focussed on helping, but staying calm to avoid causing any more fear or panic.

[Chaid?]

[*Do not worry, he is going to help.*]

"Aden, come help me. Grab the other, hurry."

I turn to find a pair of twins standing nearby.

"Um, David?"

It is the boy who is speaking. The girl stands by his side with her hand clasped firmly in his, watching silently. Her eyes flicker briefly to glance in my direction before returning to Kendra. I would wonder what is going on behind me, but am too concerned about Kendra to care to look.

"Just do it," replies the older boy, named David.

The twins are younger than Kendra, probably about nine, and both sport identical shoulder length, glossy black hair and large, piercing blue eyes with flecks of silver glittering within them.

Aden lets go of his sister's hand and moves to help David. After a few moments they manage to get both Kendra and Ashley free. Aden sets Ashley down gently and makes sure she is comfortable. There is a large purpling bruise on Ashley's forehead.

Kendra is placed gently down, David bunches up a few of the greenish foam pillows under a coat to make her a good pillow to rest her head on. She is still for a minute, calming down and catching her breath. Her eyes are locked on David. David sits down nearby and nods to Aden who moves instantly back to his sister's side.

Kendra's face is a mess, covered in clinging smashed green foam particles. She wipes the mess from her face and it comes away smeared with red. I see the gash on her forehead. It's not deep, but it is bleeding quite a bit.

She frowns, and her whole face pales suddenly, as she sees the blood smeared across her hand. A trickle of blood creeps down her forehead towards her face.

[*Kendra...*]

Her eyes widen, and her breathing grows suddenly more rapid.

[Chaid?]

She is close to panic.

[*It is only a small cut, but it is bleeding quite a bit, my dear. Bunch up a shirt or a sweater or something, hold it tightly to the cut. Ok?*]

She nods and starts looking around for something to hold to her forehead.

"Whoa, hold still ok, you got a nasty cut on your forehead," David says as he rushes back to his feet and starts to search for something to bind the gash.

"Thanks," she replies softly and then spies the group of kids trying to wake up Miss Jordan. Her eyes go wide once again, this time in shocked concern.

[Chaid, is Miss Jordan ok? She's not...]

She trails off. I half expect her to start crying, but instead she gains a fierce look in her eyes I have not ever seen before. Then Kendra's face transforms, relaxing and unexpectedly allowing her beauty to burst free and dazzle me, even through the bits of foam, smeared blood, and messy hair.

I am stunned, then shocked further as I watch the gash on her forehead rapidly stop bleeding and then close up. The line of cut flesh colours, first turning the pink of newly healed flesh, then darkening to match the natural hue of her skin. The wound is completely gone, the process only taking seconds.

[*Kendra?*]

She turns more fully towards me. By the focussed concern for Miss Jordan I still see glimmering in her eyes, she is completely unaware of what has just happened.

[*She is,*] I pause for a moment, trying to collect myself. It is difficult to do, as I reel from the revelation of such extraordinary power hidden within her, [*she will be fine. You should help Ashley, make sure she is ok.*]

She nods, glances once more back towards Miss Jordan, and then moves over to take care of the still unconscious Ashley. She moves David's make-shift pillow under Ashley's head and cleans up her friend as much as she can. Ashley is still out, but she is breathing normally and appears ok, except for the bruise.

Free to think, for a small moment, I collect my thoughts. Kendra's incredible ability to heal, a power over the flesh. It makes her skill at blending into the background and hiding her beauty, make a sudden amount of surprising sense. I believe, now, that she is not even aware of what she can do.

"Hey there, you're looking much better."

I turn to see David has returned. Kendra smiles at him, a warm smile. At this point, or even before this point, she would have faded once more into the background. She does not, and her beauty is shining brightly, her eyes a glitter. I smile a bit myself. Maybe I was never supposed to be the one to break Kendra out of her shell.

"Thanks, um... David?"

He smiles a winning smile back at her and nods, "Yeah, that's right. And those two over there are Aden and Adele."

He motions to the twins and Kendra turns to

smile at them, "I'm Kendra. Thanks for helping my friend, Ashley."

The twins smile, but only slightly and rather awkwardly. Their hands are already clasped together tightly again.

At this moment I suddenly realize why I should know who these kids are. If the Wiltshire-Ark community had a royal family, these kids would be that family's children. The heirs to the empire. Princes and princesses. I almost laugh.

I don't laugh and all the mirth in me is suddenly snuffed out as I watch David. With Kendra distracted by the twins, his smile fades as if nothing more than a decoration to be put on display whenever appropriate. His blue eyes, warm a moment ago, are now cool and observant. He tilts his head just a bit, looking at Kendra's forehead with great interest. The wadded up t-shirt in his hand drops as he studies the place on Kendra's forehead where the cut was.

David smiles again, just slightly, but enough for me to see the smile of a cat about to play cruelly with a crippled mouse. I realize then, to my dismay, that I am not the only one to have witnessed Kendra's amazing recovery.

❖ 3 ❖

"Oh come on, Chaid, you're being a bit overly anti-social, even for you!"

[*I am not anti-social, I am just being cautious and suggesting that you be the same.*]

Kendra is stuffed in the small closet of her bedroom, sorting through every article of clothing she has. She is putting an awful lot of effort into not finding anything suitable to wear for tonight's big event. She pokes her head out of the closet and gives me a glare. I can't honestly tell if she is truly annoyed with me or not.

"Why? I thought you would be happy that I am making new friends."

[*Absolutely, I am ecstatic that you are making new friends. See... not being anti-social. All I am suggesting is that you not forget old, trusted friends.*]

She rolls her eyes and the look of annoyance fades. She disappears back into the closet, still tossing rejected pieces of clothing out onto the floor.

"I can't believe..."

I can't make out the rest, her voice muffled and lost in the closet.

[*My dear, I cannot make out what you are saying and if you start yelling someone might hear you.*]

[I was saying that I can't believe you are jealous. Like I could forget you if I wanted to.]

I sigh. I could almost laugh, but I don't.

[*I do not mean me, fool girl. I mean Ashley. You know she would love to be invited to this dinner party just as much as you, if not more. That, and I would feel better if you had someone else there that we trust. Someone else to watch out for you.*]

Kendra is silent for a minute, then another. I wait patiently. This is an important night for her and I certainly do not want to ruin it. But neither do I want it to be ruined by anyone else and I still don't trust that David. He has done nothing but be kind and friendly to Kendra since the bus incident, but every now and then I catch a cold look in his eye when he is sure no one else is looking. The way he studies her has set me on edge for the past three weeks. I keep waiting for something horrible to happen, because of him.

She steps out of the closet then and, if I breathed, the sight of her would certainly take that breath away. She is radiant, and it has nothing to do with the clothes she has chosen.

[Why don't you trust David?]

There is definitely annoyance there now. Her eyes, glittering with excitement over tonight, darken as perfectly formed eyebrows furrow in just a touch of anger. It still amazes me to see her shift in this way, just as it is amazing that she still does not know what she is doing or what she can do. I meet her eyes and think carefully about how to answer.

[*Trust? Trust takes time my dear Kendra. It must be earned. Tonight you enter a world of privilege and power. A lot of power, and power can do funny things to people.*]

She is not buying it, I can see it in her still darkened eyes. There is something else there, but I can't quite read it. She is staying silent, still waiting for me to explain. I keep trying, thankful that she is at least giving me the opportunity to try.

[*I am not saying you should not go, in fact I want you to go. I want you to have the time of your life tonight, but above all else, I want you to be safe among these rich, and powerful new friends of yours.*]

It is quite a speech. I hope it is enough. She stares at me for a minute longer, the annoyed glint still in her eyes.

[So, you want Ashley to go with me so I will be safe?]

[*So you will have someone there you can trust.*]

[Ashley?]

I am confused and not understanding why she keeps getting more annoyed when Ashley is mentioned. She is thinking about bringing Ashley, but instead of taking comfort from the idea of having a good friend there with her, it is making her more upset.

[*Why would you not want to bring Ashley along with you?*]

Kendra shifts her gaze away from me and bites her lip without answering. I watch as, before my eyes, her dazzling beauty fades. Kendra, hiding herself from the world once more. Something clicks in my head and I realize what is going on.

[*Kendra, my dear, since the bus accident a few weeks ago how often has David found you so that you two can talk and hang out?*]

She turns back towards me and the beginnings of a smile are tugging at the edges of her lips.

[Almost every day.]

[*And does he do the same with Ashley?*]

She shakes her head silently.

[*Who did he invite to this dinner party tonight?*]

[Me.]

She has not yet let go of her lip, but that dark annoyance has started to slip away from her eyes and she is not fading into plainness any longer.

[*That is correct, my dear. He invited you, he is interested in you. Just you, not Ashley, not anyone else.*

Bring Ashley, please, for my own peace of mind.]

She smiles then, and just like that the annoyance is gone. She disappears back into the closet and a moment later, while she starts looking through her clothes all over again, I can hear her talking to Ashley on her phone. She invites Ashley, and I smile as a touch of relief washes over me.

❖ 4 ❖

The Hartshorn house is massive; a mansion of old grey stone and thick carpets of the deepest crimson over floors of dark, polished wood. Long hallways are cluttered with family heirlooms and strange mementoes that only members of the family would understand. Hallways lead to numerous huge rooms with vaulted ceilings and roaring fireplaces big enough to stand in. Dozens of little nooks and shadowed places hide everywhere, in which to meet and whisper.

Everywhere are the Hartshorns; a collection of families bound together in the ownership of this entire community and in the running of its businesses. Here and there are guests, all employees of the Hartshorns and permanent residents of the community. There is music, laughter, and the chatter of voices, but it is hushed and muted, as if afraid to be too noticeable. Now, if this is such an amazing opportunity to impress the bosses, why would no one want to be noticed?

Kendra and Ashley are escorted through the halls towards the dining room by a hard looking, but well dressed butler who is probably a trained soldier. I follow along and try not to let the weight of this place's mystery and hidden secrets overwhelm me.

The two girls chatter away, awed and excited by the grandeur of this place and by the fact that they are a part of it for tonight. Kendra glances behind her, just for a moment, to catch my eye and give me a wink. For the first time, she is her true gorgeous self in the presence of Ashley, and in spite of my surroundings, I find myself smiling.

The adults share a dining room that is bigger than the entire dorm Kendra lives in. The teens share a separate dining room, which is only marginally smaller.

Kendra is escorted to her seat at the long, dark wood table, her name inscribed elegantly on a brilliant-white place setting. Ashley is then shown to her own seat farther down the table instead of next to Kendra. The table has been set with great care, an equal number of guests on each side of the table and all the place settings perfectly balanced. Except where Ashley is sitting. She is seated awkwardly at the corner of the table, like her place was set up at the last minute. As other guests arrive to their seats, Ashley gives Kendra an excited smile, which Kendra returns. They are both happy and I stand back from the table, content to let them enjoy the evening.

When the first course begins to arrive, I notice that four seats are still absent. I notice too, that Kendra keeps looking at the empty seat at the head of the table. She fidgets and I wonder where David is, as she no doubt is wondering herself.

"Sorry, so sorry, for being late. Please, do not stand on ceremony and wait for your hosts, eat...

everyone."

The voice definitely does not belong to David, it's too young and seething with obvious disdain, poorly masked by politeness. I turn, along with everyone else at the table, to see who it belongs to.

He is young, younger than David, but older than the twins -Aden and Adele- who are following quietly, hand in hand, behind him. He is about Kendra's age. His hair is dark, like the twins, but cut short and has been carefully styled into a neglected, spiky punkishness that tries, and fails, to suggest he never styles his hair. He is tall, taller than David, but very thin and lanky. He does not appear to be fragile though, not in any way. He moves with a careless grace that betrays the arrogance of a wolf stalking unseen among a herd of sheep. His dark eyes are hungry, and it is unnerving as they pass over the corner I am standing in, out of the way.

Passing by the table where everyone is sitting in silence, he suddenly slaps the palm of his hand down on the table. Everyone, including myself, jumps.

"I said, EAT!"

A few of the gathered kids, even the older ones, go pale. I even hear a whimper or two. He chuckles darkly, and grins at everyone. Aden sighs and lets go of his sister's hand. She doesn't seem to notice, as she intensely studies the group of kids at the table in front of me.

"Niko," Aden says calmly, "you promised you would be civil to our guests this evening."

Niko turns, almost a blur of sudden speed, and glares down at Aden. The younger boy calmly returns the stare, without glaring or backing down.

"David entrusted you to be a good host, in his absence," continues Aden in a smooth calm voice of reason, "you don't want to disappoint him, now do you?"

Niko continues to glare and for a moment I think he is going to deck the little boy. A sneer flickers briefly across his face before he turns away and makes his way to the seat at the head of the table. He sits, looks up and over the gathered kids, smiles an oh-so-fake smile and motions for the servers to unfreeze from their spots and continue to serve the first course.

"Welcome, honoured guests," Niko says, his voice still thick with poorly disguised disgust, "Aden speaks true. I have given my word to be gracious to our invited guests, and so I humbly ask you to forgive my rudeness."

His mouth twitches, almost displaying another sneer.

[*Kendra, my dear, please steer clear of that one. He could care less about receiving forgiveness from anyone gathered at this table, or from anyone else either.*]

She doesn't answer, just nods her head absently as she continues to stare at the frightening boy. She does manage to close her mouth though.

Niko finishes up his speech as the servers step away from the table and sweep away to get the next course ready. "Please, do enjoy yourselves."

He sits and begins to eat. He scarfs down his food, not talking or chatting with anyone. He eats quietly and efficiently, methodically clearing his plate without joy. Everyone else at the table takes his cue and eats quietly. I think it is safe to say that no one is enjoying themselves.

The dinner, uncomfortable at best, continues in this way to its conclusion. Everyone exits the table as soon as politely possible, and I follow Kendra as she wanders unhappily into the maze of hallways through the Hartshorn mansion.

❖ 5 ❖

Kendra has found herself a little corner of privacy in an elevated reading corner that overlooks one of the main hallways. The walls are covered in books, a reading lamp glowing over a comfortable looking plush chair. There is very little room on the landing and it is absent of people, making it perfect for Kendra to relax in. She leans against the banister, absently watching the Hartshorns and their guests below. I leave her to her thoughts, which I know are all about David, and peruse the titles of books collected on the shelves.

"Did you enjoy dinner?"

Kendra gives a little squeak of surprise and I whip around to find that Niko has silently joined her at the bannister. He is leaning against it, just as she is, less than a foot away from her side.

"Yes, um... Yes, I did enjoy it, a lot. Thank you," she stammers out, quietly. I watch as, with each stammer and awkward word she says, her beauty retreats further away and she hides herself away once more.

A little war of emotions flicker across Niko's face, too fast for even me to understand them all. I am uneasy though, and look around to see if Ashley is nearby. I would feel better if Kendra wasn't alone with this creep.

"Good. I am glad," he says, his face finally settling on cool interest, "David asked me to make sure you were enjoying yourself."

Kendra's eyes light up at the sound of David's name. Niko's dark eyes meet her own and he smiles, though it is not entirely a friendly smile.

"Thank you..."

He waits for her to continue, then realizes she is politely waiting for him. He steps back away from her, his movement startling in its quickness, and bows just slightly towards her.

"Forgive my manners, or lack thereof. Nikodemus Davalos, of the House of Hartshorn, at your service."

He looks back up and the smile on his face warms slightly as he notices Kendra's own, somewhat unsure, smile.

She nods back to him, "Kendra..."

"Yes," he interrupts, "David has told me all about you."

"Will David be joining us this evening?," she asks, the hope clear in her voice.

He moves, again the motion startling in its suddenness, back to her side at the banister overlooking the hallway below. He glances down, dark eyes flickering among the guests and family below.

"No," he answers quietly, something in his voice that I think may be a touch of jealousy, "as eldest, David has many responsibilities to attend to. He regrets not being able to attend, but such is the burden of duty."

Niko turns to Kendra then, ignoring or just not caring about the disappointment all over her face. He studies her a moment, and she turns towards him as she becomes aware of his scrutiny.

A warm smile forms from his thin pale lips, "I can see why he likes you."

Oh, this brings quite a smile to her face. She comes out of her shell, just a bit, and the smile lights up her face. Niko's own smile grows in response and he nods his head towards the hall.

"I promised David that you would enjoy yourself, and I intend to keep my promise."

He turns back to the bannister and looks down. I move over to them, peering over the banister at what Niko is studying and find a group of teens, all guests by the wide eyed wonder on their faces, gathered below the landing. They are whispering amongst themselves, gathered closely, but I can still hear a little of what they are saying. They are talking about Niko, and what they are saying is not pleasant.

Kendra is also looking down at them, and she pales as she catches a few words of what the group is talking about. She gives Niko a quick glance, but he is still studying the group of kids, his smile still in place.

Niko slips back away from the bannister, making no sound as he does so. He motions Kendra to follow, the smile still in place across his face, though I can see cruel amusement starting to leak through.

Bending his head down towards her, he

whispers, "you're different than the others, Kendra. That's why David likes you. If I had not come up here to join you, would you join them in mocking me behind my back?"

He is still smiling, but there is no warmth left in it. Kendra does not see this, as she is too busy basking in hearing how much David likes her. She is no longer hiding herself away, a subtle shift of her features and her true beauty slowly reveals itself. She shakes her head.

"I knew it," he says, then, "wait here a moment, please."

He slips away down one of the stairs to the hallways below, a blur of silent motion, and is back only a short moment later. He has a pair of large red candles, burning steadily, taken from the hallway. Below the landing, the group of teens are still chattering away, making fun of Niko and his strangeness, completely unaware of the landing above or that anyone is near enough to overhear them.

He passes one of the candles over to Kendra, who takes it, blinking in the glare of candlelight in her face. She has no idea why he is giving her the candle, but holds onto it anyway.

"Shhhh...," he hushes, without need as Kendra is making no noise at all.

Niko turns out the reading lamp behind them, then smiles that wickedly amused smile at Kendra before blowing both candles out and stepping carefully back over to the banister.

Kendra follows, moving carefully with the candle's large pool of melted wax shifting with her every movement. Niko peers over the side, grinning, and then carefully extends his arms, with the candle clutched in his hands, out over the bannister and overtop the group below. He turns his face sideways, evil glee dancing in his dark eyes, and nods for her to do the same as him.

She hesitates and Niko's eyes darken as some of the malicious mirth leaves them.

He whispers calmly to her, "you would join them, then?"

She whispers back to him, "your promise," she pauses a moment, then continues when it is evident that he doesn't know what she means, "you promised to be gracious to your guests."

He nods in thanks to her as he pulls his hand, and the candle, back across the banister. He turns towards Kendra, the dark mirth still dancing in his eyes, and motions, with a nod of his head, for her to continue.

She meets his eyes, and as little as I like where this is going, I am curious to see what she will do. After another short moment, she doesn't turn away from him, but lifts her arms to extend the candle out overtop the group. Niko's grin widens as she starts to tilt the candle to the side.

I look over the banister, down at the group of teens, just as a crimson stream of melted wax pours down atop them. The hallway erupts in screams of pain and shock. Echoing through the hallway, only slightly quieter than the screams, is Niko's cruel and mocking laughter.

Most of the teens take off, screaming for help,

but one of them looks up in pained disbelief. Her head is covered in hot, red wax. It looks as if most of the poured wax hit her directly, and it is soaked all through her hair. I hear a whimper of pain from Kendra and glance at her. She is peering down at the red stained and burned teen, and tears start to slide down Kendra's face. I look back down at the humiliated girl below, and recognize Ashley's face beneath all the wax.

"Well, that was interesting," says Niko, his voice having lost all pretense at kindness. He starts walking away, "it shall be my pleasure to tell David how protective of his brother you were."

Just before he disappears down the stairs, he pauses and, with nothing but contempt, says one last thing to Kendra. "Welcome to the family."

Then he is gone, leaving Kendra alone with her tears and the painful sobs coming from Ashley in the hallway below.

- Chapter 4: A Boy -

"One person's lie is another's truth. The only absolute truth is that everyone chooses what to believe in, and then does everything they can to make it remain true." *– unknown*

❖ 1 ❖

We are sitting in the back of the bus, alone. In front of us, separated by only a few empty rows, are the Hartshorn kids. I don't like them much, the twins weird me out, especially the girl Adele. When she looks at Akeem she gets this very far away look, like she is looking right through him. Akeem doesn't like them either, but then again, he doesn't like anyone, not really.

Akeem, sitting and staring out of the tinted window at the countryside passing by, smiles as if reading my thoughts. It wouldn't surprise me, he has been able to read minds since he was ten and in the last three years he has gotten very skilled at it. However, he has never admitted to being able to read my mind.

Akeem is a little tall for his age. He spends most of his time alone, other than with me, and as far away from other people as he can get. This has led him to volunteering often to work at the Ark's many gardens, doing jobs that most people want no part of. He has a pretty athletic build for a young teen. His features are all shades of dark; dark eyes, dark hair, and dark skin. His hair is not that short. Instead of falling down near his shoulders, it curls thickly around his head. Though dark brown, his eyes have a strange silvery glint, as if they have the moon's reflection swimming in them. They glint even brighter when he is reading someone, which he is almost always doing when someone is nearby.

I catch, out of the corner of my eye, Adele turning to glance at the back of the bus where Akeem and I are sitting. I wonder if maybe she can read minds as well. Akeem shifts his gaze to meet her stare, glaring back at Adele and her brothers with silent contempt. After a moment, she turns away. Just another odd moment between the two of them.

[Chaid, it's... it's her...]

I have no idea what Akeem is talking about. I follow his gaze and realize that he wasn't glaring at the Hartshorns at all, but was studying someone else beyond them, near the front of the bus. The rest of the community's kids are talking to Miss Jordan. Akeem told me she was writing a novel, but keeping it secret. He also told me that it sounded pretty good, at least what he could read in her head.

[*Who or what you are referring to, my friend?*]

[Kendra, it's Kendra. It's really her, she is here with us.]

[*Seriously? Our Kendra, from the orphanage?*]

I can't believe it, not really, but he nods and I follow his intense gaze to see a pretty girl that, when I really study her, could indeed be Kendra. It's been years, but he could be right.

[*How could we miss running across her before now, if she has been living here with us the whole time?*]

Akeem shrugs and I am a little annoyed to realize that he really doesn't care. [She could be new. It happens.]

[*I suppose,*] I sigh, [*you really should try to be more sociable.*]

He snorts, dismissing the suggestion just as he has dismissed it numerous times before. I don't really blame him, it's difficult to make friends when you can hear every thought that goes through their mind; good and bad. I will continue suggesting it though, whenever I can. It is something he needs.

[You want to know how I can tell it is definitely her?]

[*Certainly, my friend. Tell me, how?*]

He turns slightly towards me, a knowing and all-too-smug grin on his face, [I heard her talking to you a minute ago,] he chuckles, probably at the look on my face, [she called you an anti-social ghost.]

I am having trouble processing what he is saying, and the first thing that pops out of my mouth is, [*I am... not... a ghost!*]

He laughs, a little too loudly, which draws Adele's knowing gaze around to us again.

[*So, just so I can truly understand what it is that you are saying, she is talking to me. But not me, as in the me you are talking to right now. She is talking to... another me? And you are sure it is indeed me, you can hear his thoughts as well? What... well, what am I saying?*]

He is about to break down and start crying, he is laughing so much. I, to be honest, really do not see what humour is to be found in the situation. It really is quite perplexing and more than a little unnerving.

[*Really, that is quite enough. Honestly, how would you feel, Akeem, to find out that there is another version of yourself out there. Think on that and then we shall see if you are still laughing so uncontrollably.*]

He is still laughing, uncontrollably.

What brings him around is the sudden uproar of the students up front. Something to do with the teacher, again, but I have not been paying attention. Then I notice that Adele is staring at Akeem again and that he has noticed this time. He is glaring back at her. This is what has calmed him down. He faces off against her, a silent contest of wills in trying to stare each other down.

It starts to quiet down up front, and the staring contest between Akeem and Adele is interrupted when her twin brother pulls her around to sit back down in the seat. In fact, all of the Hartshorn kids are sitting down suddenly.

[Oh... crap...]

Akeem's eyes are wide in sudden shock.

[... Chaid...]

He tenses up, dips his head down, and locks his arms against the back of the seat in front of him like he is bracing for a car crash.

[... something's coming...]

He doesn't get to finish as the bus is suddenly rocked by an explosion from outside, and launched into the air. Chaos takes hold of the bus as it twists and rolls in the air, and everyone inside of it is put through a blender.

❖ 2 ❖

[*Akeem, my friend, please listen to me. I am not asking questions because I do not believe you. I do, indeed, believe what you are saying. I just do not understand everything that you are trying to tell me. That is why I question, so I may understand. Do you see?*]

It is difficult for him, and I quiet and let him think over what I am saying. When he is with other people, he doesn't really need to listen to what they say as he can hear within their thoughts exactly what they mean to say. It is not easy for him to realize, truly, that no one else does this. It makes it just another frustration for him, when he is trying to talk to someone, even me, and they don't immediately understand what he is trying to say.

Finally he nods, calmer now than he was a minute ago. This is good. We are walking through the pristine hallways of the Ark. A massive superstructure housing the tens of thousands of people that makeup the entire Wiltshire community. We are on our way to crashing the Hartshorn family's party and I am not at all in agreement with his plan.

I need to collect my thoughts, question Akeem where both of us can focus, and make sure Akeem is not about to do something extremely stupid. I turn down another hallway and head towards the centre of the Ark. Akeem follows, trusting me, for which I am grateful. A few minutes later we pass through an automatic door, and get hit with a blend of rot and growth smelling humidity; one of the gardens that Akeem has worked in. It's evening, so no sunlight is left to filter down through the centre of the Ark into the greenhouse-like garden, and there are no lights to disturb the life cycle of the many fruits and vegetables growing here. It's dark and we are completely alone; perfect.

I sit down, not too far away from the door, in the middle of a gravel path. Akeem sits with me, takes a deep breath and then visibly relaxes. The fewer people nearby, the easier on him it gets, and I need him focussed.

[*Thank you, my friend. Now, first tell me about Kendra and,*] this part is awkward, [*this other version of me. Could you read him?*]

He shakes his head. [No, I can't read you Chaid, you know that.]

I don't really, but Akeem has always insisted that he cannot read my mind.

[I could read her and she was thinking about what you... the other you, was saying.]

[*That is... interesting.*]

[I have suspected for a couple of weeks, after the first time I noticed her. It's why I wanted to go on the field trip, so I could spend so much time nearby and really read her.]

I should have noticed this, but Akeem keeps a lot to himself, even from me.

[It took time, but I read memories of the orphanage and us. They were hazy and hard to find, buried deep in her mind, but she has them. It really is Kendra and she has you.]

[*Or someone like me.*]

One of his eyebrows rise, questioning. [She just happened to name him Chaid? Not too big of a coincidence for you?]

I don't believe in coincidence, so I nod my head. [*Ok, it would make sense that our Kendra would have an imaginary friend named Chaid.*]

[When all of us were young, Chaid, and together at the orphanage, you were always our friend. You were never a friend to just one of us.]

I nod. [*Thank you, my friend, but please understand how... strange... it is to find out that there is another version of me out there. It is...*]

[Strange, I know. It's her, Chaid, and we have to get her out of here. We all have to get out of here and find the others.]

[*Yes, you keep saying that. Because of what you read in the Hartshorn kids, yes? What did you get from them on the bus?*]

He shakes his head, and I can see his frustration bubble up from within. It is all over his face as he stares fiercely into the dark and beyond, with his brow furrowed.

[I didn't read anything specific. I told you, I can't really read them other than the occasional flash of strong emotion. They are somehow blocked or shielded or... something. I can't read them. The only thing I could read was a sense of knowing something was about to happen. They knew that explosion was coming, they were expecting it and they were not scared.]

[*You believe they had something to do with it?*]

He nods. [After the bus crashed, they weren't scared. I didn't read anyone outside of the bus, no kidnappers trying to get into the bus like the Academy told us, nothing until the rescue came.]

He pauses, and looks at me, almost like he is willing me to understand. I can hear the frustration in his thoughts as he says, [they were only interested in Kendra and now David never leaves her alone. I think it was a setup, some kind of test for her.]

It hits me then, what he believes; [*You are saying that I am not the only thing you and Kendra share in common. You believe she can read people just like you and they are after her power.*]

Akeem shrugs, [I don't know if she can read people, but I do think she has power. And yes, I also think they want to use her.]

Akeem stands up and so I guess the time for talk is over. [We have to get her away from them and then get out of this giant rat trap.]

I stand up as well, placing one hand on his shoulder. [*I said I believe you and I meant it, my friend. I believe and now I also understand, thank you. We will get her, and we will get out of here.*]

Akeem smiles and together we exit the garden and start heading upwards. Like all people with power, the Hartshorns like to look down upon everyone else, and so we ascend to the top of the Ark superstructure, to the Hartshorn family mansion.

[*So, if you will pardon my asking, but you do have a plan, right?*]

Akeem pauses to give me a smirk. [Time to crash a party.]

❖ 3 ❖

Crashing the party was a lot easier than I thought it

would be, so easy that I actually felt a little embarrassed for the hosts who let Akeem just walk right in. Well, to be perfectly honest, I also felt a little paranoid that any second one of the Hartshorns' hired goons was going to jump out of the shadows, grab Akeem and laughingly ask him if he thought it was really going to be that easy to sneak into their home. But that didn't happen.

Now we are in the lavish mansion and, as we search for Kendra through the labyrinth of half-lit hallways adrift with so many strangers, I realize that getting into the party was the easy part.

[Chaid, this way.]

Akeem heads off down a hallway suddenly, and I rush to catch up. It is difficult to keep up with him. As Akeem passes by, the party guests seem to unconsciously part to let him through, unhindered. They just seem to get in my way and I do not like it when people touch me. It is... uncomfortable. As I manage, finally, to make it to Akeem's side, I wonder if this is another of Akeem's abilities. He can get into people's minds, maybe he can get other people to do what he wants.

He stops, so suddenly that I almost run through him, then changes direction and rushes down another hallway. He stops before he has taken two steps, and the entire hallway fills with the anguished screams of a teenage girl.

[No... damn.]

[*What? What has happened Akeem?*]

He turns to look at me, then steps to the side of the hallway as several adults tear through to get to the source of the scream.

[One of the Hartshorns, that creepy one, just tricked Kendra into dumping hot wax on her own best friend. We should have gotten here sooner.]

No sooner does Akeem say this when the very Hartshorn kid he is talking about, the one named Niko, turns the corner and begins heading straight for us. His head is down, but it's still hard to miss the satisfied smirk on his face. He is ignoring anyone around him, walking quickly like he has a purpose. He doesn't even notice Akeem. Akeem, however, has definitely noticed him.

[*Akeem, stop!*]

I yell at him, because he is about to do something stupid. He pauses, but still looks ready to slug the Hartshorn kid.

[*Kendra! She is the one that needs you.*] That grabs his attention much more solidly. [*Right now and if you deck this moron all you will accomplish is getting yourself tossed out and then you will not be able to help Kendra at all.*]

He glances away from Niko, first towards me and then back down the hall in the direction where the scream came from. The screaming has stopped, now there is just the confused murmur of many gathered people trying to figure out what happened. Niko passes by us both at this moment, and Akeem can't help but snap his attention back to the treacherous little jerk. Before I lose him to his temper, I start to follow Niko.

[*Go help Kendra, my friend. I will follow him.*]

He still pauses, wanting to beat the snot out of

Niko.

[*Go, my friend! She needs you.*]

That finally breaks through his anger, and he nods to me and turns to head off towards the crowd around Kendra.

[Thanks Chaid. I will meet you in the garden as soon as I can get Kendra free of this place.]

I rush off, catching up to Niko and, oddly, finding myself having the same issue keeping up with him as I did keeping up with Akeem. People just instinctively move out of his way without even noticing him, then get right in my way as I try to keep up.

I follow Niko through a crisscross maze of hallways. He passes through a doorway mostly hidden behind the massive bulk of one of the hired goons, and I slip in quickly before the door can close or the muscle can get in my way. I find, on the other side, a small study, dimly lit by recessed lighting above wall to wall bookshelves. These Hartshorns certainly have a lot of books. Sitting there at a centre table, are the other Hartshorn child-royalty.

On one side of the table, sitting side by side within hand reach of each other, are the twins; Aden and Adele. At the head of the table is David, the eldest. Niko joins them, but only after travelling around the room to make sure each door is locked. He pulls a comfy looking chair over, kicking one of the table's chairs out of his way, and sits down at the corner away from the others. He can barely see over the edge of the table, and after he kicks his feet up onto the table, he can barely see anything. I roll my eyes, and am a little amused to see that I am not the only one to do so.

With a weary voice, Aden asks, "what did you do, Niko?" Aden doesn't even wait for a reply, before assuming the worst and pressing Niko with another question. "I thought you never broke your promises?"

I swear Niko almost spits at Aden, but he stops when David gives him a warning look. After a moment of silent glaring, Niko finally answers.

"I didn't mess with anyone. It was sweet little Kendra."

He pauses, and chuckles when everyone at the table looks surprised.

"You should be proud of her, we overheard a few of the ungrateful little charity-cases talking crap about me. I could do nothing, because of tonight's promise, but she... well, she really burned them..."

He trails off into cruel laughter, unable to continue. It continues until David slams his hand down on the table, startling Niko out of his laugh-fest.

"Niko, we need her," says a very calm David while he looks directly into Niko's eyes and waits for his little brother to collect himself.

"What?! You think I don't know that," responds Niko, in a suddenly pathetic whine.

David settles, his voice losing a bit of that icy edge to it, but only a little, "I know you do, Niko. I just need you to be careful is all. I don't want you to push her too far too fast. We can't lose her."

This gets nods of agreement from everyone around the table, Niko included. Wait, not everyone. I notice Adele looking around at her brothers, not nodding, uncertainty and confusion passing over her face.

She sighs, and then quietly asks, "why?"

Everyone snaps their attention to her, disbelief in their eyes. Everyone erupts into talking, all at once. Aden is trying to talk calmly with David trying to talk over him, and Niko just starts shouting. Most of the words Niko shouts are obscenities and insults.

Finally, David slams his hand down on the table, and yells, "enough!"

Everyone quiets, though Niko continues mumbling partially under his breath until David gives him an icy stare.

"I'm not saying it's wrong, David," says Adele in a voice that sounds too wise and too weary to belong to an eleven year old child, "I just want to know why we are spending so much time and effort on this one girl."

David nods, and sits back down. Everyone else follows his example and they settle back down into their chairs. All eyes at the table are on David, waiting for him to speak.

"Power, Adele. It's all about power. She has it and we need it."

But Adele is not buying it and she shakes her head, "House Hartshorn has plenty of power, David."

"Yes, power others are always trying to take away from us. Someday, not too distant into the future, it will be up to us to run this House. We have an opportunity, right now, to gain some security for the future and I believe it would be foolish to pass it up."

Niko is nodding his head, a lot, in agreement. Even Aden seems to be in silent agreement with his brothers, but Adele peers questioningly at her oldest brother.

"You believe? You do mean that it's what Father believes? It was Father who told you to bring this Kendra closer to the family, right?"

Oh, this is getting informative, and despite the odd looks and challenging staring contests between Adele and Akeem that have always annoyed me, I am finding that I respect her awareness. It is clear by the look on her face and the tone of her question, that she no longer believes it was their Father who put David up to this. However, what gives me pause is the look on David's face; one of sudden confusion and doubt.

"I... yes he... he," David stumbles over his words, stuttering a bit as he tries to collect himself, and the shocking contrast between the normal David and this confused David makes me wonder who it was that really influenced David into manipulating Kendra. I almost wish I could pull up one of the plush comfy chairs in the study, to listen further. Akeem is going to be most interested in hearing what I am finding out.

Finally David collects himself, his siblings having waited patiently, and he says, "I don't know. It..."

I have no idea what David says then. That I miss what he reveals is most disturbing as it hits me then that only something of immense power could influence one of the Hartshorn princes within their own home. I miss it because Akeem's voice suddenly fills my head with an almost screamed, [CHAID!]

He has never been able to speak to me over distances before, but I don't get a chance to react, or respond. I don't even get a chance to move as I... blink... and am suddenly somewhere else. It is disorientating, being somewhere and then being somewhere else without knowing how or why. It's never happened before, but I realize that I am standing beside Akeem, like he summoned me to his side, and we are still in the Hartshorn mansion. Kendra is standing on the other side of Akeem, his arm wrapped protectively around her.

I am about to say something, somewhat angrily as whatever Akeem has done to make me appear at his side has cut off my opportunity to find out who or what is really trying to mess with Kendra. I keep silent as the full strangeness of the situation becomes apparent to me. All around us are people from the party, except they are frozen in place.

❖ 4 ❖

They are not frozen, not really. They are just standing there, not moving, staring at Akeem and Kendra. A collection of Hartshorn servants, hired protection, and party guests, all standing near motionless, their eyes fixed upon my friends. I notice then, with a chill creeping along my spine that threatens to make me shiver in rarely-felt fright, that a few of them have shifted silently to stare at me too.

"Akeem, what... what is going on?"

Kendra is frightened and still attempting to recover from whatever she did to her best friend before Akeem was able to get to her. Her pretty face is puffy and flushed from crying, her cheeks still wet with the half dried remnants of her tears. She shrinks away from the stares of those around her, and -unless my eyes are playing tricks on me- she actually does physically shrink away and become shorter.

Akeem grabs hold of her hand, and moves himself in between her and them. They do not react. They do nothing but continue to stare.

"I don't know, don't worry Kendra, they won't hurt you," he responds, but there is worry in his voice.

[Chaid, I can't read them.]

[*Calm yourself, my friend, and concentrate.*]

[I can't, there is nothing to read from any of them.]

[*You mean you are blocked, like when you try to read the Hartshorn brats?*]

I realize, by what he says next, that he is close to complete panic and we are in some serious trouble

[No, I mean I could read their minds one moment and the next moment their minds were gone. Completely and absolutely gone. There is nothing here to read. I have no idea what is staring at us right now.]

"Akeem? What is wrong with their eyes?"

She is right, their eyes are dark, in deep shadows that make it difficult to see them clearly. As I look within them, I get the uneasy sense that I have seen, and should know, what is behind their eyes. Something cold, featureless, empty, and hungry... very, very hungry.

I feel myself drawn in by them, everything else around me begins to fade and I start to feel the hunger behind their eyes. I feel it within me, I feel hungry, and I'm afraid of that hunger.

"Kendra," Akeem whispers as I try to shake myself out of whatever curse has been cast over me.

[*Akeem... run...*] I manage to stammer.

"...run."

[*RUN!*]

He doesn't even finish the single syllable in the word run, before the possessed crowd moves. Possessed; it is the only way I can describe them. Like some powerful entity has hollowed them out and filled them back up with its own singular will. They don't move like a group of people, they move all at once, all at the same time, all just limbs of the same single monster. And they move without making a single sound; in utter alien silence.

They rush forward and overwhelm Akeem and Kendra, crowding in and around them. Both of the young teens are, within seconds, lost to each other and me. I can hear, muffled and indistinct, Akeem yelling in anger and Kendra screaming in fear. The possessed still make no sound, like a bad movie on mute.

I can't do anything to help them, I can't see them or get to them or save them even if I could find them in the swarm of possessed. I am useless. Several of the possessed turn, quietly but still as one entity, and start to move towards me. They... It is staring at me, right at me, as they... It moves in and I am getting crowded and overwhelmed. I can't hear Akeem or Kendra any longer, and I have nowhere to go as the swarm of possessed close over me and everything starts to go dark. The last thing I feel as I go out is that cold, bleak, and endless hunger as it suddenly rushes through me from within. Then I am gone.

❖ 5 ❖

My eyes open to nothing, a nowhere, where I am alone. Then I hear wind, chilling me. I feel a soft ground beneath me, my face resting in it. It is like a powder. I try to get up, and cannot move. There is no light, but I begin to see through the murky nothingness. A flat plain of grey powder that goes on forever.

Later, I don't exactly know how long later as time seems to have stopped, I try to move again. I put a whole lot more effort into it, as I can hear something other than wind, something not good. Footsteps, moving my way. Long shambling steps; whatever is making them is slowly dragging itself across the ground. They are coming straight for me, without hesitation or care. It, whatever It is, is coming for me, and I can feel Its hunger.

I still can't move.

[*Akeem?*]

I call out to him, but hear nothing but the wind, the long dragging steps continuously getting closer, and now the sound of Its rasping breathing.

[*Akeem... please...*]

Nothing.

[*... help?*]

It gets closer.

[*AKEEM!*]

It grabs hold of me, and tosses me into the air and I land, roughly, on my back in the grey powder.

I would be amazed and possibly even intrigued if I wasn't so terrified. It actually grabbed hold of me, I could feel It and It could feel me.

It is a rag wrapped bundle of stick-like limbs in the guise of something humanoid. Grey-silver strands of hair, coated in layers of dust, fall from the shroud of rags wrapped around Its head. Its face is lost in shadow and hair and rags, but Its oh-so-very hungry grin is very plain to see. Sharp, stained teeth. It looks at me, the grin widens more and more, impossibly wide and full of more teeth. I want to be anywhere else.

"You..."

By all that is good and merciful, It can speak. It only says the single word, but it is enough. Its voice is liquid filth being poured into my ear.

I close my eyes, I look away, I try to stuff my ears with the grey powder beneath me. It howls, enraged, and one skeletal-like hand, tipped in black talons, reaches out and plunges into my chest. Its howl is lost to my own, and the agony is endless.

The pain is less. Its hand, covered in some inky blackness that has come from within me, raises one long finger and waves it back and forth in warning.

"Listen," It speaks once more and I wonder if the pain might be preferable to Its foul words, "you... cannot... save... them..."

I hear the words and I grab hold of them, cling tightly and use them. I forget the pain, I forget the tainted feeling I get from listening to It speak. I ignore the pain and terror and give It my full attention and now calm gaze. It is staring back at me, daring me to speak. I manage to smile, though it probably comes off as a grimace, but as I smile I also lift up my own hand and give It a gesture of my own.

"I will never stop trying!"

It howls in rage, lifting Its face up towards the empty sky above and away from my middle finger. I laugh, though I'm unsure if It will hear me over Its own howls.

[*Farewell my friend. Take care of Kendra and the others, should you also find them.*]

Everything goes dark.

❖ 6 ❖

I open my eyes and am surprised to discover that I still exist. Or do I? Everything still remains dark and I have no idea where I am. I look around wildly to see if I am still trapped in that awful place with that awful thing, but calm down as I realize that I no longer feel that horrid, endless hunger. I don't know where I am, but at least I am not in that place.

[Chaid!]

I am only too happy to hear Akeem once more and start to become aware of my surroundings. I realize that it's so dark because I am in some kind of concrete tunnel.

Akeem and Kendra are both there, sitting on a ledge running along the side of the tunnel. Below them is a river of thick, slow moving sludge; some kind of waste system. Akeem is staring at me with eyes wide in surprise.

[*Akeem, my friend. I am very happy to see you once more. Where are we, and what happened?*]

"Akeem, Chaid is back. I can see him!"

Kendra pulls away from Akeem and smiles, but she is not looking in my direction.

"He's back for me too," replies Akeem.

It's still weird, to know another me is standing unseen, to me, not far away. I wonder if he just went through the same thing as I did.

Kendra takes a few steps away, clearly concentrating on talking with her version of me. Akeem steps closer to me. He is wearing outdoor clothes, like the day of the field trip. There are a couple of packs nearby. What is going on?

[You scared us a lot Chaid, we didn't know if you were gone for good!]

[*Not if I can help it, my friend. When those people swarmed, everything just went sort of black for me. How did you and Kendra escape? And where are we?*]

He smiles, and I can see he is remembering that night as his eyes get a far away look in them.

[You should have seen her, Chaid, she was amazing! I was right, she has power, but it is not like mine. She has control over her own body. When they swarmed us, she bulked up with muscle, like out of nowhere, and just mowed them down. Pulled me to safety and we ran. It wasn't until we got out of that place that we noticed that you were gone. That was three days ago.]

Three days!

[*That,*] I pause to collect my thoughts and recover from the shock of having been gone for so long, [*that is most extraordinary. I cannot apologize enough for not being there for you, my friend.*]

He smiles. [Just glad your back.]

I look around once again, still not sure where we are. [*So then, my friend, please explain to me where we are and why we are here and what is going on?*]

[Of course,] he turns back towards Kendra. She is already putting her pack back on, so he joins her and they prepare to head out, [we are escaping from the Ark.]

Just like that, escaping, like it's something that is done every other day. It does explain the waste system we are in at the moment. I imagine that a superstructure the size of the Ark would have a massive network of sewage and waste disposal tunnels leading through, down, under, and out of the Ark.

[*How?*] I ask.

Akeem turns back towards me, and I see the cheerful excitement of my return has faded to a look of seriousness. It is... not... something I expected, but it looks good on him. On them both. He takes Kendra's hand and then begins to walk down the tunnel, using a powerful flashlight to illuminate their way.

[The tunnel systems, doorway access codes, and entire security and surveillance system layout is all in my head now.]

He taps his forehead and then smiles at Kendra who rolls her eyes and gives him a quiet giggle. She must be explaining the exact same thing to the other me.

[It wasn't too hard to find the right people with the right information, and read it from them. So far it has worked perfectly. They know we are missing, but anytime a patrol gets near us, I read them and we avoid them.]

He has a grin on his face, a very pleased-with-himself grin with no little amount of arrogance in it. This is the Akeem I know, but I am suddenly amazed to see it soften as Kendra gives his hand a squeeze.

[It's still tricky. These tunnels are dangerous, but the couple of times we were in trouble, Kendra used her amazing abilities to save us.]

[*That is good to hear, my friend. So, once we get out, where to?*]

Akeem frowns and his brow furrows with a little annoyance.

[*Please, my friend, do not mistake my question for disapproval. It was long past time for us to make our exit from that place and those people. I was merely curious.*]

Akeem stops, pulling Kendra to a stop, and addresses me out loud, "I don't know where we are going to go. I don't even know if it will be any safer out there than in here with the Hartshorns. I only know that we have to get out."

Kendra gives his hand another squeeze and adds, "and find the others. We are stronger together."

I nod to them both, knowing only Akeem can see me, but assume the other me is also nodding his approval of the plan.

Akeem's brow furrows suddenly, as his eyes get a far away look I know too well. Flecks of silver glint in his eyes.

"We have to move, they are nearby. A large patrol."

He pulls Kendra's hand and we all hurry down the tunnel, with Akeem leading us away from the

Hartshorns and towards the outside world. It may not be towards safety, but it is definitely towards freedom.

❖ 7 ❖

We almost make it. Two days of running and hiding in the underbelly of the Wiltshire-Ark's filth and stinky sewage. The further down we went, the worse and more gross it got. The longer we made it without being caught, the bigger the patrols got and the more often they would block our escape route.

"They're on to us," Akeem is leaning against Kendra as she half carries them down the filthy tunnel. His eyes are rolled way back into his head, slivers of white showing between not quite closed eyelids. He sounds tired.

"How do they know where we are?"

Kendra sounds tired too. I am worried.

"I don't know! I can't..."

Akeem trails off, and suddenly his eyes are wide open in alarm.

"The Hartshorns are with them." Akeem doesn't sound tired anymore, now he is scared. "That's why I can't read them anymore. It's Niko, David, and the twins; they are hunting us down."

Kendra pauses, but says nothing. She doesn't have to say anything, the look on her face says it all; she has given it her all and has next to nothing left to give. The look on Akeem's face mirrors her own.

[*NO! No, we do not give up, my friends. We do not!*]

Akeem snaps up, like being woken up from a bad dream and gives Kendra a look. They give each other this look; this powerful affection that is developing between the two. They embrace and begin whispering fiercely. I don't hear what they say, nor am I meant to. Nor would I intrude to. What passes between them is for them alone. I am glad for them both, for this connection between them gives them strength; a faith in each other, a confidence in themselves, and a resolve to save each other.

They split apart, reluctantly, or start to when Kendra suddenly yanks Akeem close to her and kisses him. I look away, giving them a moment of privacy.

She heads out to the front lines of the coming battle, taking position in the middle of the tunnel's walkway. Akeem slips away from her and finds a small corner to wedge himself in, out of the way and ready to give her support from where he can safely concentrate.

[*It is remarkable, my friend, how well you two work together after knowing each other for so little a time.*]

Akeem doesn't get a chance to answer me, but I catch a glimpse of an almost dazed smile on his face.

"Kendra!"

It's David, his voice echoing down the tunnel.

"Come on, Kendra. I'm not angry and you're not in trouble, I just want you to come home, please."

Smooth bastard. I don't like this, so I move past Akeem and Kendra and follow David's voice to see what I can scout out for my friends. I wish I could do more, but at least in this way I can help.

I find, not far away and still quietly moving closer to my friends, a squadron of guards armed with strange bulky rifles. The Hartshorn kids are indeed with them, with David in the lead and Niko by his side. The twins are safely in the back of the group. Aden has his eyes closed, concentration flickering across his face. Adele just stares over and past the guards, looking down the tunnel, through me and towards my friends. I do a quick count.

[*Akeem, if you can hear me, all four of the Hartshorn fiends are here, with about a half-dozen armed security guards. They are advancing towards you. Prepare yourself, my friend.*]

"Kendra, please," David again, the perfect amount of concern in his voice, "I'm worried about you."

[Thanks, Chaid.]

I hear Akeem, like he is still right next to me. I smile and start to turn away in order to head back to my friends, but something stops me. Adele suddenly turns to her brother and whispers frantically in his ear. He nods in my direction, in the direction of Akeem and Kendra. Niko follows Aden's nod, turning around to face in my direction with a wickedly eager grin on his face. The guards move forward.

David leads on, "Kendra, I," his stone cold face giving nothing away while his voice still carries the perfect amount of worry and care.

"Please, I miss you!"

I turn then, hoping that she is not buying it, and race ahead of the patrol to make it back to my friends first. I am pleased to see that both Kendra and Akeem are still waiting, ready to defend themselves, even if it is a last stand.

David comes around the corner first, and alone.

His face has come alive, portraying the same worry and care that his voice has. He doesn't get a chance to say anything.

"GO TO HELL!," screams Kendra as her body ripples and swells before everyone's eyes. It's unbelievable to witness. In moments her clothes are several sizes too small for her and she is almost unrecognizable, now looking more like a junior miss weight lifting champion.

She charges and David, a momentary look of utter shock that is the first honest look that I have seen on his face, stumbles away from her. The guards charge around the corner of the tunnel, past David, and towards Kendra.

Three of the guards go down to one knee and bring their rifles to bear on Kendra, while three more guards do the same thing, standing behind and overtop the first three kneeling guards. Six rifles track Kendra as she charges towards them. I see trigger fingers begin to twitch, then all six of them drop their guns and collapse to the ground, holding their helmeted heads and yelling in agony.

I smile as Akeem shows them that reading minds is not his only trick. [*Burn them, my friend, scorch them until their thoughts are burnt black!*]

David steps forward, Niko trailing only a step behind. As David passes the guards, they each stop yelling and start to recover. David stops just in front of them, his arms held out like he is waiting for a hug from Kendra. She is still charging, and David just waits for her to come to him. The guards are getting their act together, apparently now shielded from

Akeem's mental assault.

Then, in a blur of impossible speed, Niko dashes in front of David and leaps at Kendra like some kind of wild animal. She jumps, her entire body pivoting like an acrobat. As she and Niko meet, her hands flash out and grab hold of his slender frame. She flips over and past him, sending him twisting past her. Kendra lands, and keeps charging without losing a single step, while Niko disappears over the railing with a howl that cuts off suddenly with a splash into the sludge below.

David lifts his hands up higher as Kendra bears down on him, her distorted lips pulled back in a grimace of anger. David waits, ready, and the six soldiers are just starting to track her again when Akeem steps out of the shadows, his eyes squeezed shut in concentration. He stumbles towards David and the others, and I see a thick stream of crimson pour from his nose and flow down his face.

A yell of outrage and pain grabs hold of my attention and turns me back around towards the patrol. David has stumbled down on one knee and Kendra is flying through the air once more, this time aiming a perfectly executed flying kick like out of some kind of kung fu movie. It is aimed right for his face, and does not fail to connect.

With a crack that sounds out at the same time as the sharp snap of six rifles being fired, Kendra kicks David in the face, snapping his head back and sending him sprawling to the concrete floor. Kendra doesn't land, but tumbles to the ground as six very large tranq-darts have speared her torso and have already flooded her body with toxins.

She rolls across the ground, stops, and does not get back up.

Akeem screams, falling to his knees with blood pouring freely from both nostrils now. All six of the guards begin screaming again and fall back to the floor. Only Aden and Adele are not sprawled out on the floor in some way, both of them watching the fight with horror and shock frozen on their faces.

Everything goes quiet then and I turn back towards Akeem to find him dangling in Niko's grasp. The tall, lanky boy is dripping in sewage, but is still grinning from ear to ear as he holds Akeem in the air with both hands wrapped around Akeem's neck. Akeem's face is already turning blue, even while more blood pours down his face from his nose. With a sadistic chuckle, Niko gives Akeem a rattling shake and then tosses him through the air, to tumble into Kendra's prone body.

No. I can't believe it. I can't do anything about it. I want to scream, yell, punch, fight, attack, burn, detonate, and destroy, but I am helpless and all I can do is scream in helpless rage.

The soldiers are slowly waking up, but most are still too overcome by Akeem's attack to do much more than sit unsteadily against the wall and wait until the world stops spinning. David is back on his feet, sporting a nasty bruise still blooming across his face. I am surprised his nose isn't broken. He is angry, and for a moment I think he is going to kick Kendra's unconscious body. She is slowly deflating from her enlarged and empowered form, diminishing until the everyday Kendra is left. She does not move, other than the shallow rise and fall of her chest as she struggles to breath.

Akeem lies still on the ground, tangled with Kendra. David points at them and barks at one of the guards to secure them. At the sound of his cold fury, Akeem stirs slightly and lifts his head to glare at the Hartshorns. It lasts only a moment before Niko slams his foot against the back of Akeem's head and once more my friend falls into unconsciousness.

Defeated, I sit down next to my friends and wait and wish for them to recover. David barks at the guards a couple more times, but none of them are yet ready to do much of anything. Finally, muttering in disgust, David yanks a set of cuffs and restraints from one of the guards and passes a set to Niko.

"Niko, secure the mind freak. Make sure the hood is secure. He won't be able to see and the headset will pump his ears so full of distortion that he won't think clearly for months."

Niko catches the set of restraints, chuckling, and steps towards Akeem. David opens up another set of restraints, a wire mesh of cuffs and chains and collars that look like they will wrap Kendra in a cocoon of steel.

Just as the two reach the tangled pile that is Kendra and Akeem there is a sudden... blink... and a strange young girl appears, crouching next to Kendra and Akeem. With blazing red hair and a roguish grin, the girl waves a finger at the frozen-with-shock Hartshorns.

"Tisk, tisk... You fellas don't play very fair..."

She giggles, grabs hold of Akeem and Kendra, and with a... blink... they are gone.

I can't believe it.

Everything starts to fade to black.

The last thing I hear is David screaming in absolute rage.

I am gone.

- Chapter 5: Silver -

"Looking for the silver lining in everything makes you a fool willingly choosing ignorance over understanding. Life is pain, a struggle, so open your eyes and fight! Then again, they do say ignorance is bliss." – *unknown*

❖ 1 ❖

She reaches out, without needing to look, wraps her hand around the hilt and settles her perfectly manicured and delicate fingers across the worn leather weave. It is a hilt that has felt the skilled grip of numerous masters over many long ages. I watch in awe as her fingers flex almost imperceptibly, reading the hilt, and then settle into the perfect grip. Light and confident, she makes the weapon an extension of her arm, an extension of her will.

With only the whisper of supreme sharpness cutting through air, Onshuuko draws the blade free of its scabbard. Without hesitation, without fear of failure, and without nicking the blade against the scabbard, the blade weaves its way free. Around her pivoting body the blade blurs and comes instantly to rest at the end of a powerful iaijutsu -single strike kill- maneuver.

All is silent. All is still. Onshuuko remains poised, motionless, slightly crouched with her sword arm outstretched and the blade pointing just past the wooden practice dummy. The small crowd of observers -her sensei, father, and fellow students among them- watch in unmoving silence.

A moment passes, then another, and no one breaks the silent stillness. Then the wooden dummy emits a wooden creak. I watch. I would hold my breath, if I breathed. I would chew my nails, if they could be chewed. By the looks of the crowd, many of them are doing this for me.

What I don't do, would not dare do, is speak to her. I wouldn't, for anything, disturb her concentration. Nor would I desire to turn those jade green eyes of hers, glinting with cold anger and hatred, upon me. I remain silent, and wait.

Another moment and the wooden dummy shudders slightly, all too easy to miss unless one is watching for it. I hear a few of the observers draw a sudden breath.

The top half of the dummy crashes, suddenly, to the floor. The lower half remains still and unaffected, the dummy cut clean in two.

Her eyes never leave her sensei.

Before the top half of the dummy can finish tumbling to a rest upon the matted floor, Onshuuko reverses the blade in a blurred spin and snaps the sword back into its scabbard with perfected ease. Her eyes remain upon her sensei, even as she bows deeply in respect to him and her father. The old master of the sword returns her bow even as the impressed crowd claps politely and begins to murmur amongst themselves. Her father turns away to speak with someone of importance next to him. He does not bow, nor is he clapping.

I catch a glimpse of icy anger glitter in those

enchanting eyes of hers. She turns with a swirl of graceful precision, and stalks away, leaving the crowd behind. I glance at the crowd before I follow her, and see her father watching her leave. It is for just a moment, but I see something there in his eyes. Something immense, something powerful, something foreboding, and something that I have been seeing in his eyes more and more often of late. I wish I knew what decision he was trying to make about her, and that it didn't fill me with dread.

❖ 2 ❖

The table sits about knee high, carved out of a single piece of dark wood. I don't know what kind of wood, but it's very beautiful. Ornate carvings of fantastic creatures cover the entirety of its polished surface. Slender serpent-dragons are entwined around each leg. A proud dragon-lion roars from one side of the table, while a phoenix spreads its flaming wings on the other. The wise face of a dragon-tortoise studies the room from the head of the table, its grand shell forming the tabletop.

The table is the only thing in the small, but spacious room surrounded by rice paper walls. Bleached a pristine white and framed in slats of bamboo, the walls depict a repeating watercolour pattern in black, white, and greys. A crane, forever frozen in mid step, stands in a pool that reflects a crescent moon shining over a distant castle of ancient ruin. The crane holds no interest in the castle, which looks to have once been mighty and impressive. It is a sad painting, beautiful and lonely. I have caught

Onshuuko staring at it numerous times, though she refuses to admit she likes it.

The wall behind me hisses open, pulling my attention around and away from the wall painting. A family servant shuffles across the shiny bamboo floor to place several plates of food upon the table. Immediately, other servants follow and place other dishes down around the table. Each servant is dressed in a simple white robe and pants. They make no noise at all, going about their chores quietly and efficiently. Their bare feet are silent as they cross the floor.

A moment later the Oshiro family enters, mostly ignoring the servants who deftly slip out of the way. Each servant bows their head as the Oshiro family passes. Mr. Oshiro enters first, a tall and solidly built man of tanned skin and steely grey hair. Whether he doesn't see, or chooses not to see, his servants is unknown to me, but he passes without any sign of acknowledgement. Following behind is his wife, a demure beauty many years his junior. She returns the servant's bows, politely, but coldly. Their son, Isao, follows with a smile on his eternally cheerful face. He is only five, but has already learned to keep his silence in the presence of his father. Still, he manages to keep his cheerful disposition even while respecting his father's preference for quiet. He bows, always with a smile, to everyone. Last, and trailing far enough behind that a few servants have to scuttle back to their bowed postures of respect, is Onshuuko. She gives barely a hint of a bow to each servant as she reluctantly follows her family to the table and its meal.

Tall for her age, Onshuuko stands almost eye to

eye with her mother, but has already surpassed her mother's beauty. She moves with a grace and refined precision, every motion deliberate and practised. Wide, jade green eyes see everything in an instant. Just as quickly, the mind behind those enchanting eyes judge the worth of everything she sees.

Her gaze passes over me and I feel myself bow in respect without thinking about what I am doing. I feel the full fierce weight of her judgement fall upon me as she pauses to glare. I know that look all too well, telling me that she finds me unworthy of her attention. She continues towards the table, ignoring my presence. I manage not to sigh this time, I guess I am getting used to it.

The Oshiro family members take their places around the table, bow to each other, Mr. Oshiro bowing the shallowest, and then sit. Everyone waits, quietly, as Mr. Oshiro inspects the food, finds it presentable enough, and begins to eat. Then, and only then, do the rest of the family begin to eat.

Thus is another meal shared among the Oshiro family. They have lived in accordance with very old and very sacred family traditions, passed from generation to generation for a very long time. Even with today's modern world of advanced tech, the Oshiro home is an echo of their past. It is not something that seems likely to change, nor something Mr. Oshiro would allow to be changed. Family and tradition are everything to him, and so he has made sure that they are everything to his family.

"Father?"

Everything stops, everyone pausing in the

middle of their very carefully polite eating to glance up. Isao and Mrs. Oshiro both look first towards Onshuuko and then towards Mr. Oshiro. Isao glances back towards his older sister. As Mr. Oshiro pauses in his own meal and directs his severe gaze towards Onshuuko, Mrs. Oshiro quickly directs her gaze back down towards the table and her meal.

"Onshuuko, finish your meal," he replies back to her in a calm, but firm tone.

Onshuuko dips her head, returning to her meal, but I catch a glimpse of icy anger glittering in her eyes. Isao continues to stare at his sister for a moment before a soft tap on his shoulder, from Mrs. Oshiro, redirects his attention back to his own meal.

Later, as the meal is finishing up and servants are beginning to take empty plates away, Onshuuko looks back up, her eyes calm once more, and looks back towards her father.

"Father?"

No one reacts in surprise this time, knowing she wasn't going to keep her silence for long. I do catch a subtle sigh from Mr. Oshiro. I quickly glance towards Onshuuko and see a glitter of anger renewed in her eyes as she also notices the near silent sigh from her father. It doesn't dissuade her.

"Yes, daughter, what is it?"

She meets his eyes, not an easy thing to do for anyone let alone a 13 year old girl, and holds his gaze.

"I would know, father, if you were pleased with my performance."

It's not quite a question or request, but more a demand for an answer. His slightly furrowed brow shows everyone that he is well aware of this.

"Your sensei has made it well known how impressed he is with your progress," he replies with an icy tone of finality.

She ignores his tone, as she often does, and presses him further. "Sensei says my potential is not yet fully tapped, that with further training I..."

She does not get to finish, cut off suddenly by his increasingly icier tone, "I am fully aware of what your sensei says, daughter. He and I will speak further about the proper course of your future."

He stops speaking, fixing her with a stare full of annoyance and near-outrage. It is almost a dare for her to speak again, and I shake my head as I foresee the downward spiral approaching. I am not the only one, both Mrs. Oshiro and Onshuuko's brother keep their heads down, staying out of the argument about to blow up.

Mr. Oshiro begins to rise, as if the conversation is over and resolved. Onshuuko rises with him, which immediately causes him to stop and glare in true outrage at her.

Her fine eyebrows furrowed in an anger that mirrors his own, she glares right back, "My future, father. Should I not be included in such..."

Again he cuts her off, his voice increasing in volume as his anger continues to increase. "You will do as you are told, daughter..."

This time it is Onshuuko who cuts him off and I can't help cringe. "But I want to..."

Mr. Oshiro slams his hand down onto the table, causing even its sturdy bulk to shudder and the plates to rattle across its surface, "SILENCE!"

There is quiet for a moment as the two of them, father and daughter, glare at each other in mutual anger and disappointment. I see Onshuuko's lips part just slightly as she draws in a breath. He sees it as well, and he cuts her off before she can even start to speak.

"Should you value having any future, daughter," he says, quiet, calm, and oh so very cold.

I hear Mrs. Oshiro draw a sudden, sharp breath, her eyes wide in shock.

Mr. Oshiro ignores his wife and continues, "you will cease your disrespectful insolence at once. Your future has been a gift to you, from me."

He reaches out, grasps one of Onshuuko's arms, and pulls her close to him as his voice dips to a near whisper. "And it can be taken away, should I choose, now that..."

This time it is Mrs. Oshiro who interrupts, reaching out and laying a hand lightly upon her husband's arm, and I don't know who at the table is more surprised.

"Akihiro, please stop..."

And then he hits her.

It happens so fast that, if I had to ever blink, I would have missed it. Mrs. Oshiro's face is jolted sideways by his hand and she catches herself against the table. Silence and shock reign across the table as everyone stares, unbelieving. Her face reddens immediately, a mixture of shame and physical trauma. Onshuuko, arm still firmly held in her father's grip, stares in stunned horror.

Mr. Oshiro glances around the table, a look of disgust upon his face. His mind is a billboard that I can too easily read; he lays the blame and responsibility upon his family instead of rightly taking it upon himself. He drops Onshuuko's arm, almost flinging it away from him, and silently leaves the room. Servants scatter out of his path.

At the table, Mrs. Oshiro sits still as silent tears slide down her still blazing-red cheeks. The silence is finally broken by Isao beginning to cry quietly, his endless-seeming cheer finally broken.

Onshuuko rises. She begins moving around the table towards her brother, when Mrs. Oshiro gathers him into her arms and shoots Onshuuko a glare that causes the young girl to stagger away in renewed shock and pain.

"Mother," she says.

In a small, pained voice that almost makes me pity the woman, Mrs. Oshiro replies, "leave us... just... go," and hugs the sobbing form of Isao closer to her, shutting Onshuuko out.

Her eyes still dry, but closer to tears than I have ever seen them, Onshuuko turns and leaves the room. I, being the faithful shadow I am, follow silently at a respectful distance.

❖ 3 ❖

"Hai!"

The loud, sharp yell is followed by an almost simultaneous sharp "wack" as Onshuuko's wooden practice sword hits the solid dummy figure. The sound echoes across the garden, rebounding back to us and then starts to fade.

Onshuuko doesn't move the entire time, her entire focus set upon the wooden dummy and her practice blade resting against its throat. I can't help but imagine the dummy's head rolling across the grass if she had a real blade. I wonder if she's imagining the same, or perhaps someone else's head.

It remains silent for a moment longer after the echo fades, before it's broken by Isao's tentative voice, "Onshuu?"

Her grip upon the sword tightens for just a moment, then relaxes and she slowly pivots in a graceful arc to face her little brother.

His almost always present cheer is still missing, but his wide eyes are hopeful and I am not sure if this is good or bad. I watch, with interest.

Onshuuko, her eyes still guarded, crouches down and lays the wooden practice sword upon the ground. She doesn't smile, but reaches out a hand towards Isao.

"What is it, little monkey?" she says quietly.

The little boy rushes into her, wrapping his arms around her neck and burying his face in her shoulder.

"I'm sorry," his voice muffled and nearly lost to me, "I'm sorry they were so mean to you."

Onshuuko resists, her arms trembling for a moment, then they wrap around her little brother and hold him close. She says nothing. I move away from them both in order to give them their privacy, so I don't get to read the reaction in her eyes.

Isao hugs her for a minute more before letting

go and stepping out of her embrace. He wipes his eyes and then composes himself, giving her a very formal and deep bow.

"Forgive me, sister. I did not mean to interrupt your training. Please continue."

Her eyes widen at this and, without realizing it, she cracks a smile at her little brother. I am both amazed and impressed with the little guy's skill. He smiles back, that near unquenchable cheerfulness blazing forth once more.

Onshuuko rises, wooden sword in hand, and returns his bow before turning back to her practice. That smile still upon her face, and with Isao following in her footsteps, she begins a series of practice kata across the garden. Soon all I can hear are the wooden swishes of the practice sword sweeping through the air and her sharp kai shouts.

I watch, still off to the side and out of their way. Onshuuko falls further and further into her routine, her focus narrowing to an amazing degree and enhancing her skill until every movement she makes is perfected precision. Isao stops suddenly, his eyes wide in surprise. Onshuuko continues through the kata she is currently working on, not noticing that her little brother has stopped.

I watch Isao rub his nose, shrug and then run ahead to catch up to his sister. I realize, suddenly and shockingly, what has happened; Onshuuko almost hit him. The dull wood blade of her practice sword swinging so close to his nose that he could feel it. He is too close to her, too excited, and too interested in her amazing skill with the sword that he is not staying far enough away. And she is too engrossed by her training exercises to notice. Even now I can see him running to catch up to her, heedless of the danger.

And I don't know what to do.

[*Onshuuko!*]

I say it without thinking or meaning to, but now it is too late. She has heard me. With a sneer of contempt she turns towards me, her lovely face transformed by her hatred.

[Hold your tongue, demon!]

Bitter words, angry and disgusted. I am expecting them to be this way, have felt their sting before, but they still rip through me like wind born razors. It doesn't stop me though.

[*Onshuuko, please do be...*]

I don't get to finish. She raises the wooden blade into the beginnings of another kata, this one designed to kill.

[Shut up, foul demon!]

She finishes her kata with a savage downward slash that almost hits Isao across the head as the blade sweeps back behind her. She still has no idea he is so close to her.

I point behind her, [*Isao is...*]

She cuts me off, emitting a guttural scream of rage and charging towards me. The wooden blade sweeps the air in front of her as she sprints across the garden. I watch as Isao launches into a sprint behind her, thinking it is just another of her kata. He struggles to keep up to his sister, but is managing to succeed. They both have no idea of the danger.

[*Onshuu...*]

"Demon, shut up!"

She is screaming out loud now, completely heedless of her surroundings.

[*Isao is...*]

"Don't you dare speak his name!"

I start to back up as she gets closer and closer.

[*But he is...*]

"You do not even think about Isao!"

[*I only want him...*]

"Demon, I will kill you!"

I can't move fast enough, not backwards and probably not even if I turned around to run properly. Her rage fuels her, propelling her forward towards me.

[*Apologies, Onshuuko. I only meant to help, please!*]

I fall to the ground, but scatter no pebbles of the garden path. I am insubstantial, nothing but a phantom. I do not fear her practice sword, but I do fear her hatred and anger. I fear that she will hate me so much, so intensely that it will destroy me. I glance around, taking in the sight of the beautiful garden, wondering if it will be the last thing I see.

"DIE, DEMON!"

"ONSHUUKO!"

I hear Onshuuko skid across the pebble strewn garden path, coming to a halt over me. I cringe, waiting for her to strike me down, but nothing happens. The sudden tense quiet makes me open my eyes. She has turned away from me, and is staring at her father. Mr. Oshiro is standing in the doorway to their home, staring in horror at his daughter.

Between them, Isao lies unmoving in the grass.

"Isao!," she cries out.

Dropping the practice sword she rushes forward with tears in her enchanting green eyes. Her father reaches the boy first and steps between Onshuuko and her brother, causing her to bounce backwards off her unmoving father. She looks up at him from the ground, unbelieving, with eyes filling with that blaze of anger I know so well.

"Father!"

"NO!"

He steps back, still keeping himself facing her, watching her, making sure she stays away. He carefully picks up the little boy, who is unmoving in his father's arms.

"Isao," she says quietly, pitifully, as she sees the rising bruise on his forehead. She was so busy attacking me, she didn't even know she hit him. I didn't see it either.

"NO! You have done enough, too much. It ends now, it is over. You... you are over!"

Each word like a slap to her face, her cheeks redden deeper and deeper as he speaks. He carries Isao back towards the door. Each step he takes away from her brings more tears flowing down her face. Mrs. Oshiro is at the door, weeping, her eyes glued to the motionless body of her little boy. She takes Isao from Mr. Oshiro and disappears into the house. Mr. Oshiro slowly, steadily returns to stand over Onshuuko.

She does not see him, sitting in a collapsed heap upon the grass and staring at the spot where Isao fell.

She says, more to herself than anyone else, "I'm so sorry, little brother."

And like thunder following lightning, her father roars at her, "he is NOT your brother!"

She snaps her head up, locking gazes with her father. But she says nothing, just stares through the tears.

"You are not Oshiro. You are not my blood," he looks at the small section of flattened grass where he lifted Isao up from the ground, "nor are you Oshiro in spirit."

Her head dips in shame and sorrow. She says nothing, but stares at where her brother had fallen. Where she hurt him.

Mr. Oshiro's voice loses much of its steel, sadness and regret creeping into it. "You will be going away to finish your education at a private school."

"Where?," she whispers.

"Anywhere but here," is his reply.

"And when I have completed my lessons at this school?"

He has already started to turn away from her in order to return to the house where his wife and son are, but he pauses to answer.

"I care not."

And then he leaves her in the garden, alone. Alone, except for me. She cries for a time, but I do not offer my comfort. I know she wouldn't accept it, even if I did offer.

❖ 4 ❖

The pale moon, full and mist shrouded, has risen high in the night sky and Onshuuko has not yet moved from the spot where her brother fell.

The flow of tears has come to an end, but her lovely eyes are still red and swollen. She has pulled her legs beneath her, folded into a meditative pose and has remained here for hours in quiet contemplation. I say absolutely nothing and I make sure to stay out of sight.

During the stretch of silence I can't help but study her, this slender girl of coiled fury. Tall and beautiful, a fierce spirit within her that blazes through in every word she says and every action she takes. A cascade of long straight black hair frames her face and falls over her shoulders to about the middle of her back. When she dips her head forward, even a tiny little bit, her face disappears behind a curtain of raven-black hair.

I am startled when, without warning or turning around to look at me, she speaks.

[Tell me, demon, why do you haunt me so?]

I am speechless.

[Can you not tell me what sins, committed in past lives, have condemned me to this cursed existence?]

I still have no words. Never have I heard her speak this way, especially not to me. Then again, she has just been exiled from the only family she has ever known, so I shouldn't be surprised it has brought about such a change in her.

She stretches, every motion graceful and

deliberate but lacking in that fiery passion that is so normal in her. I wonder if it has been extinguished.

[*Onshuu...*]

[DON'T,] she interrupts me, that fire still most definitely still there in her, but then gives a deep sigh before continuing, [do not speak my name.]

She lifts herself up from her sitting pose just long enough to twist around in order to sit facing me.

[Please,] she asks in a much more composed manner, [just answer me. I must know why it is so necessary for me to suffer so. There must be some reason, some justification?]

I nod to her before speaking once more, still not sure how to have a conversation with this girl that has hated me and shunned me for so long. I want so much to not mess it up.

[*I have not cursed you, nor do I have any desire to see you cursed or believe you are deserving of such a fate.*]

She shakes her head, sending that cascade of dark hair to whip about her face for a moment before settling once more, [no... I know you did not curse me, demon.]

She pauses, rising to her feet before meeting my gaze fully. I find it difficult to concentrate, caught up in those eyes of hers.

[You are my curse. You ruin everything.]

It takes me a moment, a long moment, to even realize what she has said. Then it hits me, and it's the nearest to a physical sensation I have ever felt. The weight of her words; I feel them sucker punch me in the guts, doubling me over in pain and wanting to throw up. Like I could.

[Can you not even answer my simple question?]

She is standing over me, the moon hanging over her shoulder, and her hair falling over her face until all I can manage to see is her shining eyes. I am trying to recover, but the pain is staggering. She has hurt me many times, but this is worse.

[*Onshuuko, please...*]

I trail off without thinking about it, and realize I had expected her to cut me off again. She doesn't, but she does continue to glare at me. After a moment she sighs and raises her arms. I notice, now, that the wooden practice sword is back in her hands.

[You, demon, are pathetic... sad really, and I think it is long overdue for you to leave me in peace.]

[*ONSHUU...*]

I barely have the first syllable of her name spoken when the sword begins to move, and I don't manage to finish before it finishes its arc and impales me. Over two feet of wooden blade plunges into my chest, through my heart, and bursts out my back.

It's real, I can feel it. No illusion of pain, or pain that is really only on an emotional level, but real true pain. It's real and I am dying.

Onshuuko lets go of the handle of the sword and steps back, her beautiful eyes wide and shimmering in the moonlight. The sword stays where she has left it; buried in my chest.

[Farewell, demon, back to hell with you. I hope you burn for an eternity!]

The last thing I feel is the sensation of falling and more and more agony. And then everything fades to black.

❖ 5 ❖

I awaken in flames. Burning around me, above me, through me. Nothing but fire! After an extremely long moment of frantic panicking, I realize that I don't feel it. I am on fire, but am not burning. My chest still hurts, but the sword is no longer buried in my chest.

I am so confused.

"IIIIISSSSSAAAAOOOO!," comes a wailing scream from somewhere not too far away.

I realize, with no little amount of shock, that I am not dead, not in hell, not destroyed, not banished, not... whatever would happen to me if I was gone. I am still in the household of the Oshiro family, and it is burning down around me.

As I come to this realization, I hear someone screaming for Isao again, and realize that it is Onshuuko. With no fear of the flames, I rush through the burning building to find her.

I find her wrapped head to toe in soaked towels and blankets, a cloud of steam billowing around her as the heat vaporizes the moisture that is protecting her. Her face is hidden beneath a white porcelain mask that is holding more soaked towels in place to protect her face. The mask is familiar, plain white polished porcelain. It is one of the favourites in her collection. I can just make out her jade green eyes within the folds of soaked cloth, wide and searching frantically for her little brother.

The heat is unbearable, or so I can tell by the rapidly drying edges of her outer layer of towels.

Even now they are beginning to singe and brown towards a burnt black finish. She won't last long if she stays in this inferno, but I find myself wondering if I should even care.

[*Onshuuko, please let me help you.*]

Who am I kidding, of course I care. I am a fool and in pain, but I care. I speak to her calmly, not expecting anything other than scorn, but unwilling to just give up on her.

"YOU!," she screams as she whips around to glare at me. The fire in those eyes is almost enough to rival the flames surrounding us.

I bow, respectfully, to her, [*yes, me...*]

Right on cue, she cuts me off, [you did this! Why won't you just die, demon!]

[*No. This... LET ME SPEAK,*] I reply, yelling before she can interrupt me again and then continuing as she is silenced, [*this is not my doing. You banished me, and now in your time of need you have called me back. Let me help you or let me go. Choose, and choose quickly before everyone pays for your indecision.*]

She is not at all relieved to see me, and for a moment I wonder if she is going to "kill" me again. Finally, however, she nods.

[Bring me to my brother, demon.]

I bow once again to her, but quickly as many of her towels are completely dry now. I take another glance, a closer glance, and notice the curling black edges of the towels as they are beginning to ignite. I pause, and then make my decision.

[*This way, my dear.*]

I lead Onshuuko quickly through the burning

hallways, seeming to know just when to turn, when to pause, and when to move quickly through the flames and falling debris. I move as fast as I can, but it is a big building and it is about to completely collapse. The heat continues to increase, and every now and then I can see Onshuuko pat out flames that are beginning to break out across her towels.

I stop at a set of screens, both partially on fire already, and step immediately to the side. Without hesitation she steps forward, past me, and kicks the screens in. Smoke erupts back out through the sudden hole, blanketing us in darkness, and I lose sight of her in the swirling chaos.

A pair of hands reach past me, gloved in heavy fire resistant material, and when they pull back they haul Onshuuko along with them. I follow, through the smoke and out past the doors to the outside garden where a security team has gathered to fight the blaze and give medical attention to the survivors.

Mr. Oshiro stands just outside of the doors, holding Onshuuko in his arms. Mrs. Oshiro is not far away, watching with tear soaked eyes as the family home is consumed by the flames. Onshuuko is clutched tightly to him, her arms around his waist and her eyes closed tightly. It would be a touching moment if his own eyes weren't open wide in shocked horror as he realizes it is Onshuuko in his arms instead of Isao.

Isao is nowhere to be seen.

With a wail of heart wrenching, soul crushing despair, Mrs. Oshiro collapses to the ground. She remains there, screaming at the burning building. Mr.

Oshiro doesn't just release Onshuuko, he pushes her to the ground and backs away, his eyes still wide in disbelief and horror as he looks at her.

"Father, I tried..." she stammers in anguish, but he just raises his trembling hands as if to ward her away, and turns away to join his wife.

Mr. and Mrs. Oshiro huddle together before their engulfed home while their servants and employees mill about in stunned confusion. The Oshiro home is consumed by flames, now a grave for the Oshiro's only truly begotten child.

Onshuuko watches, pulling the ruins of burnt black towels from her. She takes care with the porcelain mask, its bright polished surface now smeared by ash and covered in a web of heat-inflicted cracks. She stands, the mask dangling from her grasp.

She is a mess; much of her hair burned away, holes scorched through her clothing, with many red blotches of burnt skin showing. Her eyes are worse, unharmed, but their usual fierce glimmer is now broken.

With deliberate slowness, Onshuuko turns towards me and walks over. I do nothing, but wait. She does not yell or scream, and this surprises me.

[I trusted you, demon, and you betrayed me.]

[*He was already gone, Onshuuko. I would not have let you be lost as well.*]

[And you lie.]

[*Everyone lies, when they must, to protect those they love.*]

[No...]

I cut her off, [*your father did.*]

She flinches sharply, as if slapped. I take the moment of silence to continue.

[*He hid that you were adopted in order to protect you, because he cared. Until he no longer cared, and then he hurt you with the truth.*]

She recovers from my words and meets my gaze fully. I can see, within those lovely jade green eyes, a spark of her fierce spirit attempting to reignite.

[Hurt me with truth, as you are doing now?]

[*No, my dear, these are truths you already know.*]

[So you're not here to hurt me.]

I step back away from her, bowing deeply, but keeping my eyes always upon her. [*My dear Onshuuko, I am here to protect you.*]

She nods, and says, [I understand.]

I am surprised, having expected much more of an argument, or even of being once again impaled.

[*That is good to hear, my dear, and far too...*]

She cuts me off, [I understand, demon, that you are here to prolong my life... only so that you might prolong my suffering. I shall endure your presence and let you protect me only as long as I must. Until I discover a way to burn you out of existence once and for all.]

She turns and begins to walk away, turning her back on me, turning her back on her former family, turning her back on her former life. She picks up a backpack stashed behind a nearby tree and slings it over her shoulder. She pauses a moment and looks back towards the remaining Oshiro family, then reaches back behind the tree and pulls out a sword.

Involuntarily, I take a step back away from her.

I realize that it is not the wooden practice blade. I don't rush to her side, after all she ran me through before and I don't doubt that she can run me through again. Wood, steel, or other; she will still hurt me with any blade she wants.

It isn't the sword her sensei allowed her to use. A fine practice blade of metal, but she still handles it carefully and with great respect.

She turns away from what used to be her home, then disappears into the darkness of the wilds.

It takes me a moment to recover, or perhaps I am still weary of that blade. I glance back at the gutted ruin of her old life and then turn back towards her. I follow, to remain by her side and quietly perform my duty. She is protected, even if she would rather not be.

I protect her.

❖ 6 ❖

The night is not yet over, darkness clinging to the low-worn mountains, woods, and fields we travel silently through. In the far off horizon a reddening glint of the coming sunrise promises a fine day for travelling... if we hadn't just spent all night stumbling through the wilds and jumping at every sound.

"Student," calls out a solemn voice in the dark ahead of us. A voice that we both recognize instantly.

The compact form of her sensei steps out of a shadow and bows respectfully to his student. I can see her tense, but only for a moment before she responds in kind. Her bow is deeper than his, lowering her head farther in respect for her elder. Her eyes, however, never leave his. One of his first lessons she learned quickly.

"Master, you surprise me. I did not think to see you again," she looks around to the relatively remote wilderness we are in, "especially here."

"Nor did I believe I would ever find the need to be here." He follows her gaze, taking everything in with those oh-so-very-sharp eyes of his, and sighs before saying, "a dangerous place, a path for the foolish to prove themselves?"

She stiffens, but does not give a biting retort. Instead she absorbs his words and gives them her full consideration. She may have left her old life behind, but this man is still her sensei.

"Every path provides opportunities to prove one's self, master."

One of his eyebrows rises in surprise. "You wish to prove yourself a fool?"

Her eyes, a glitter within their jade depths, shift to me and I'm afraid.

"No master, not a fool," she stares at me still, "cursed perhaps and in need of purification..."

She finally turns her eyes away from me and I feel their weight lift away and free me of their clutches. Her voice softens, growing more concerned as doubt clings to her.

"... or redemption... or..."

His eyes, dark and piercing, shift away from her and suddenly I find them on me. Not looking in my general direction or looking past me. He is staring directly at me as if he sees me, and now I am very afraid.

"I know all about your curse, Onshuuko."

She trembles. He has never addressed her by her name before, at least not directly to her. It is a rare sign of respect and adoration. Eyes wide in shock, and -to my own dismay- hope, she steps towards him.

"Master, you know?"

"Yes," he replies, "I know of your shadow."

"Then," she stumbles over her words in the rush to speak everything going through her mind, and has to pause to collect herself, "then you must know how to destroy it? To banish it from me."

She actually points directly at me, "send this thing back to hell and..."

"No," he calmly says, interrupting her.

She stops, eyes going suddenly cold. There is no anger in them though, which is what I would normally expect when she is interrupted. There is suddenly a strange glimmer in them and I realise she is on the verge of tears. She says nothing in response. What could she possibly say in response to her sudden glimpse of freedom being crushed with one word.

"Student," he says, after giving her a moment to recover, "this burden is not mine to carry. As you say, it is an opportunity to prove yourself. This is not a lesson I can teach you, student. You must learn it on your own."

After a moment, she nods, and bows once more to her sensei. Her eyes dip away from him this time, and she quickly slips her arm across her face to wipe away any remnants of tears that might still be clinging to her face.

As she rises from her bow, she is startled to find him resting in an attack pose. His blade, the master's blade, is drawn and held in his relaxed, expert grip.

I didn't even hear it being drawn.

I am sure Onshuuko is just as surprised as I am, but it does not show upon her face in any way. In less than a blink of her eyes, she has stepped back into a mirror of his own attack stance, her own blade sliding free of the scabbard without a whisper of sound.

They face off, motionless and scrutinizing one another for any sign of weakness in body, mind, or soul. He bars her path, setting himself as an obstacle. An opportunity.

She faces her master, ready. Nothing shows within her eyes but pure determination.

I step back, more than once.

The moment, both of them ready and judging each other, stretches on. The tension builds as they both wait for the other to break and make the first move.

Finally Onshuuko's sensei shifts ever so slightly in his stance. She responds instantly and they attack nearly simultaneously, in silence.

I blink involuntarily, almost missing it, and it's over.

Her sensei is down on one knee, arms raised with his blade held in the palms of his hands. Onshuuko is poised over him, her own blade frozen just shy of his neck. It takes me a moment to process what has happened. He is offering her his own blade. She has just managed to hold her strike from killing him.

He doesn't move, meeting her gaze and

continuing to offer her the great honour of his sword. I see her arm tremble, ever so slightly.

"Today," he says quietly, and dawn has indeed broken over top of the nearby mountains, "you are student and I am master no longer. Take what belongs to you, Onshuuko, and go find your truths."

She pulls her blade away from his neck, sheaths it, and reaches out to take the ancient sword from his hands. She doesn't ogle it like a child with free reign in a candy shop, but grasps it reverently and instantly bows in deep respect to her former sensei.

He rises, bows in return to her, then brushes the dust from himself. Turning away from her, he departs without another word. There is nothing more that is needed to be said between them.

As Onshuuko leaves, ignoring me as usual, she leaves her old practice blade buried in the dirt. I follow, glad she hasn't yet buried it in my chest, as we drift into the wilds of the world.

- Chapter 6: Gold -

"Common courtesy, common ground, common knowledge, common values, common sense... nothing is common, not in this age, not anymore." – *unknown*

❖ 1 ❖

Dear God, it's me, Nathaniel. I would like to give thanks to you for all your wonderful gifts to me. I give thanks for my adoptive guardian, Mr. Jude, for he watches over me and guides me, without whom I would be lost. I give thanks for my home, Little Haven, and the many families that live here and have accepted me and made me feel welcome. They are, under your grace and guidance, good people. I give thanks for showing me how to be a good boy. I am a good boy...

I pause in my reading, my brow no doubt furrowed in a troubled look. I glance away from the prayer journal and see Nate sprawled across his bed with a gamepad in his hands. The boy is young, but already tall with a mane of golden hair spilling around his face like some kind of halo. Bright blue eyes shine from a handsome face currently set in a look of intense concentration as he plays some fantastical video game against one of his friends. It's not his gamepad, so he is probably playing against Johnny. Johnny is always lending Nate his toys.

I turn back towards Nate's open prayer journal and find the phrase that stopped my reading.

I am a good boy...

I can still make out the words, beneath the

pencil scratches where Nate tried to scribble that line out. A space away from the scribbled out line, Nate continues writing.

I try to be a good boy. Thank you God, you are good. I love you. Amen.

I sigh, and turn away from the prayer journal, knowing I shouldn't be reading it anyway. Nate doesn't like anyone looking at it. It is private, which only makes me worry more when I catch glimpses of Nate's innermost worries that he is not a "good" boy.

I shuffle toward Nate as he clobbers Johnny at the shooter game they are playing. A grin on his face as he racks up points causes my worries to fade for now, and I chuckle a little to myself as Nate laughs in mischievous glee. Johnny has been defeated once again, and already Nate is loading up a new level.

It is impressive to watch the boy work with the unfamiliar techno-gaming-gadget. It's another new model that I have never seen before, nor has Nathaniel, yet he handles the device like a pro. He manages the interface intuitively and the device responds so quickly to what he wants that it seems almost like it is reacting preemptively. But, of course, that is impossible.

I watch closely, as Nathaniel begins the next game, his hands swiping across the touch pads to control his in-game character. My imagination seems to run wild and I have to pause to blink and clear my mind. For a moment it seems like the device is reacting to the very slightest of motions from Nate's hands. I step back to shake the foolishness from my mind. It's just a gamepad, it can't read minds, that's just stupid.

"Nathaniel?"

I jump, startled, but Nate jumps much higher. The dropped gamepad skitters across the bed and drops with a thud on the floor. Nate, involuntarily, glances in worry at the gadget, but then returns his gaze to Mr. Jude. There is fear in Nate's eyes and I do not like it.

Jude silently holds his hand out, palm up. Hanging his head in shame, Nate retrieves the gamepad and hands it over. I can just make out Johnny's voice asking Nate what happened. Jude raises a thin eyebrow and Nate reaches out to trigger the power button. The device flickers and goes dark, and Nate hangs his head even lower. It's not a look that suits his face, and I like this even less. My earlier concerns resurface.

Jude stands silently over the boy, his dark eyes boring into the down turned boy's head. They glance over and spot the open prayer journal. It takes Jude only a moment to read the entry and he turns back to Nate.

Quietly and calmly, but still full of judgmental scorn, he says, "you will try harder, Nathaniel, to be a good boy?"

Nate nods his head, the mane of hair whipping about as the boy nods forcefully. Jude reaches out and lifts the cover of Nate's prayer journal, letting it fall closed with a snap that causes Nate to flinch. He turns back to the boy, who still hangs his head.

"Tell me how," Jude asks in his scornful voice that makes me want to grind my teeth apart and spit the pieces into his face.

Nate shuffles his feet, trying to think around the fear and shame being heaped more and more upon his shoulders.

"Nathaniel?"

Always so damn calm and condescending.

[*I am sorry father.*]

"I am sorry father," echoes Nate in a very small, very frightened voice.

[*I will not accept any more toys that you disapprove of.*]

Nate snuffles a bit, but manages not to let loose any tears, and continues to repeat my words, "I will not accept any more toys that you disapprove of."

Jude nods and shifts his gaze once more towards the prayer journal. He reaches one hand out to tap the cover lightly. I don't have to coach Nate this time, it being obvious what Jude wants said next.

"I will spend more time in prayer."

Mr. Jude nods. "Good. And for your punishment?"

This is the stupidest question you can ask a kid. It is not a question one asks, expecting a good answer. It is more of a form of mental torment. It is a cruel question to ask, the only purpose being to delight the tormentor for being so cruel.

There is no good answer, no real answer at all, so I say nothing and hope Nate also remains quiet. I try not to let the image of me breaking Jude's nose distract me too much.

"You have nothing to say then?" asks Jude.

Wisely, Nate shakes his head quietly.

"I see," replies Jude, "we shall have to arrange something fitting then."

There is a sudden and startling snap and crackle of breaking technology. I whip my head around to see Nate lift his head in shock. The gamepad, probably a very expensive gamepad, is slowly crushed in Jude's grip. Metal warps and bends, the screen shatters to falling pieces, and there is a sizzling noise as the power source is crumpled. A bit of smoke leaks out of the destroyed gadget as internal bits fry. Jude releases the gamepad and it falls with a clunk.

"Clean this up," Jude says, this time with just a touch of anger in his quiet voice.

Nate nods, but I catch something else glittering within his eyes. Anger. It is brief, gone already, but it was there.

"You will return this to your friend's parents and find a way to work off your debt to repay them for its destruction. When you are done you will explain that you are not to be friends with their son any longer."

Nate's head hangs once more and I can hear him sniff back more tears that are threatening to spill down his face. Crouching suddenly, Jude grasps Nate's chin in a bony hand and lifts until Nate is looking directly into the man's face.

He speaks so quietly that I almost can't hear him, "do you believe this to be a fair punishment?"

Nate looks back at his foster father, meeting those dark eyes for a long moment and then finally nods as much as he can with his chin caught up in the man's grip. Jude releases Nate's chin, stands and turns to leave the room without another word. Nate watches him go in silence, and I see that anger rise once more into the boy's eyes. I nod to myself, glad to know it is there, but I don't tell him it belongs there. I know he won't listen. Not yet, but maybe someday.

❖ 2 ❖

[Chaid, are you awake?]

[*I am here,*] I reply.

And it is true, I am here, though a moment ago I could not tell you where I was or even if I was. Do I sleep, or just blink out of existence? Whatever. I manage to ignore the philosophical questions surrounding my existence and walk over to where Nate is sitting on his bed. He is staring out of the open window. Outside the night is clear, the sky ablaze with starlight.

Nate seems to be looking at the sky and beyond to the sweeping expanse of stars, but his eyes are unfocused and even farther away than the stars. He is looking within himself, and is troubled. I can see as much within his eyes.

[Am I a bad person, Chaid?]

I am stunned and Nate takes my silence in the worst possible way.

[That's why God sent you, to watch me in case I do something awful.]

He is nodding slowly, sorrowfully.

[*Nate, God did no such thing.*] I pause to make sure he is fully paying attention. [*I am here to do one thing, and that is to protect you.*]

Nate ponders this for a moment, then turns his head to look at me. I wonder, often, what he sees when he does this. What do I look like? But it is only an idle curiosity, right now I am more interested in whether or not he is going to accept my words.

[Like... like a guardian angel?]

He asks, and I have to take a minute because the first impulse I have is to laugh. I don't feel like an angel, but right now is not the time to be making light of Nate's questions. I collect myself, maintain my composure, and nod.

[*Something like that.*]

[So, I am not a bad person?]

[*Of course not.*]

He frowns, his face scrunching up in a look of intense concentration.

[Then why do I do bad things?]

I sigh.

[*There is nothing wrong with wanting to play games with a friend. Games are good for you, they help develop your mind.*]

He nods, [I know that. I mean disobeying Mr. Jude and making him angry. That is bad.]

[*Nate, my friend, Mr. Jude is always angry. Why? I do not know, but I do know that it is not your fault. You are not the cause of his anger.*]

For a long moment Nate stares back out at the stars in silence. I wait, wondering if he will accept what I am saying.

[Chaid?]

[*Yes, my friend?*]

[If I am not bad, then...]

He trails off, afraid to finish. I wait patiently, and quietly for him to work up the nerve to complete his thought.

[... then why do I feel so wrong inside?]

[*Wrong inside how?*]

[I feel broken. Incomplete, like something is missing and I don't know what it is, but it is bad.]

[*I do not know why you would feel this way, my friend, but what I can say with one hundred percent certainty is that you are not a bad person. Whatever it is that you are missing within you, it does not make you a bad person and I promise that I will help you find whatever it is you need to feel complete. Ok?*]

He nods, and I take some comfort from the little bit of a smile appearing on his face. I wish I could wrap an arm around his shoulders and give him a hug, but he does seem comforted. With a yawn he lays down on his bed.

[Thanks, Chaid.]

[*Anytime, my friend. Now get some sleep.*]

He nods, and closes his eyes.

I wander back to the darker corner of the room and sit down to ponder his words. He is asleep within minutes and already I have decided what he needs to feel complete. Long after he has fallen asleep I remain in the corner of his room, trying to figure out how to get him out of Little Haven and away from Mr. Jude.

❖ 3 ❖

The fair is going well. Everyone of the Little Haven community, who is not away on a trip of some sort, has shown up. The large back lawn of the Church is busy with people, kids, tent-shades, food, and chit chat. Father Mat and Mr. Jude weave through the crowd, each going their own way to make the rounds with the community's residents. Although Father Mat is officially the community's spiritual leader and guide, Mr. Jude has long since taken it upon himself to guilt anyone he can into doing what he views is the "right" thing.

The two men chit chat and hob nob and socialize with the community. Mat leaves his flock feeling better, welcome, and more light hearted. Jude, however, leaves a wake of people feeling uncomfortably guilty for no reason they can discern. He is such a dick.

I have not yet figured out how to get Nate out of here, but I am more convinced than ever that I have the right idea. It won't be easy. Little Haven is a small gated community far from the urban blight the country's cities have become. Surrounded by dangerous wilderness and a manned wall to keep the community safe from that wildness, all access into and out of the community is securely guarded. It may not be easy, but I certainly will not be giving up.

I look around and realize that I have lost track of where everyone is. I close my eyes for a moment and when I open them I am standing next to Nate once again. Always a nifty trick when trying to find your only friend.

The fair is not too far away, Nate is hanging out with Johnny and Kira just inside the huge hedge maze that takes up the entire centre of the community. It is the most bizarre thing I have ever seen, a huge hedge maze with entrances in the backyard of every house. There are even tunnels that cross under the community's only road, so that the houses on both sides of the circular road connect to the maze. Strange.

"No, listen Johnny I'm not going to let you take the heat for this. Ok? I will talk to your parents and tell them the truth. And I will pay for it, somehow."

I turn my attention away from the stupid hedges around us and tune into Nate's voice. I catch Johnny shaking his head in response.

"But why? Seriously Nate," Johnny says, "I won't get in trouble and you won't have to work stupid chores to pay my parents off. Just let me tell them I broke it, they won't care."

Nate smiles, a pleasant smile of gratitude. "I know Johnny and thanks, but I do care. I broke it and I will take the heat for it. Besides, your parents are too cool to be too rough on me."

I watch both Johnny and Kira smile, Kira's gaze lingering on Nate.

"I broke it. It's only right that I pay for it." Nate smirks at Johnny. "I'll probably end up doing most of your chores, but I will pay them back."

Johnny snorts, but chuckles a bit. Kira, still admiring Nate's honesty, blinks suddenly and frowns. Her voice, when you can hear it, is lovely, but soft. It's like she rarely gets a chance to use it, and as I think of it, I can remember hearing her speak only very rarely.

"Nate," she says, making sure the two boys are quiet before she speaks, so they hear her, "how did you break it? You're usually so careful?"

Oh crap. I watch Nate's face go from smiling

and content to frowning and tense. Now he is going to have to lie and that's not something he does well.

"Um," he stutters, "well I..."

[*I had to use the bathroom so bad that I left it on the bed and...*]

I don't get to finish, Nate shoots me a very quick look of disbelief and disgust. He covers it up with a horrible impression of a cough. I guess it would be a horrible story to tell to the girl he has a crush on.

[*Ok, try this then. Jude asked you to help him with something downstairs and you forgot it on the bed. When you got back to your room you were so excited to get back into the game that you jumped on it. Do not forget to add that you were stupid.*]

Nate goes with my story. They buy it, and I don't miss the gaze that Nate and Kira both share, that lingers a bit too long before Johnny has a chance to roll his eyes and break it up. They head back towards the fair and enjoy the Sunday festivities with the rest of the residents of Little Haven. I hang back, studying the hedge maze and wondering why anyone would put this thing here. And also wondering if I might be able to use it to get Nate out of Little Haven.

❖ 4 ❖

The fair does well, pulls in a good amount of money and Mr. Jude seems to be happy as he begins to organize and count out the cash. Father Mat shakes his head, only very slightly, but I catch it. I slip back outside to see where Nate went, and find him back near the entrance to the hedge maze. Only a few stragglers are left now that night has fallen. The backyard of the church is well lit with several lamps, but it is late and everyone has started to head home.

I notice then that Nate is not alone and there is a good reason for him to be in the shadows of the hedge maze. He is with Kira. I smile and hold myself back from going over, respecting their privacy.

It is only a few minutes later that, to my dismay, I see Mr. Jude has no such sense of respect as he stalks angrily towards them.

I close my eyes and concentrate, opening them to find myself right next to Nate. Kira is close to him, with her hand on his shoulder but they are not kissing or anything. Nate shoots me a glare, but I cut off any angry words he is about to shoot my way.

[*Nate, forgive my intrusion, but Mr. Jude is on his way across the yard.*]

He glances over his shoulder and sighs as he sees I am right. Jude is halfway across the yard already, and very obviously upset.

"What is it, Nate?" asks the oh-so-quiet Kira.

He grabs her hand and turns toward the yard, pulling her along with him.

"Nothing Kira, it's just late and I wouldn't want your parents to worry. I did promise them that I would make sure you got home at a reasonable time."

She smiles, nods and squeezes his hand as they start walking across the yard. Mr. Jude, unfortunately, alters his direction to cut them off. I can tell, by the tensing of his shoulders, that Nate also notices.

"Nathaniel," Mr. Jude says in a curt, but calm voice.

Nate and Kira both stop and turn politely

towards Jude, Kira smiling pleasantly to Nathaniel's foster father.

"Yes, father?," replies Nate.

"What is it you think you are doing?"

Kira frowns, and glances towards Nate. She doesn't understand what kind of person Jude really is or how much trouble Nate is in right now.

Nate smiles, attempting to put her at ease, as he replies, "I promised Kira's parents that I would see her safely home. I was just about to walk her there."

"You have chores to complete, right now."

"Of course, chores that I will complete when I return," replies Nate in a very polite tone of voice that still manages to completely shock Jude and it takes a moment for the man to recover. I would be cheering and laughing if I didn't think it was about to get worse.

Mr. Jude's facade of calm composure starts to break apart as his anger surfaces. His brow furrows, and it takes a moment -a moment in which Kira is visibly getting less and less comfortable- for the man to unclench his jaw.

"Nathaniel, your chores, now. I will escort the young lady home," Jude says, his voice barely maintaining its calm.

Jude reaches out and grabs hold of Kira's arm and starts to pull her away from Nate. Nate stands there, caught up in a conflict between how much he cares for Kira and how much he fears Jude. While he is caught up in his indecision, Jude pulls Kira further away from him.

[*Nate, you promised to see her home.*]

Kira looks back at Nate, a bit of fear in her eyes

as she softly says, "Nate?"

Nate snaps out of his confusion, and says, "no, father. I made a promise and I'll not break it."

Mr. Jude is not at all impressed and continues to pull Kira away from Nate.

"I told you to go start your," Jude starts to say with menace in his voice, but is cut off by Nate.

"No!"

It is the first time that Nate has ever raised his voice to Jude, and I quietly applaud him.

Jude stops, his eyes wide and jaw clenched hard enough that I can't help but imagine his teeth cracking apart. Nate holds his ground against the man's enraged gaze and immediately steps toward him when Kira suddenly whimpers. She tries to pull away from Jude's increasingly painful grip on her arm.

Nate meets his foster father's gaze and says in a very similarly calm and disturbing voice, "let her go, now."

Before Jude can react, and by the look in his eyes he is about to react in a very abusive manner, every lamp in the backyard suddenly flares shockingly bright. They cause everyone remaining in the yard to pause in confusion or fear, and shade their eyes. It only lasts a second, then they all shatter in a cascade of sparks and broken glass. The yard is plunged into darkness, several people crying out in surprise and fear.

Nate never breaks eye contact with the man. In the sudden darkness I'm not sure, but I may be imagining a spark of blue-white light flickering within the young boy's eyes.

Jude releases the girl, who moves to Nate's side.

"I expect," Jude says, his voice fully returning to his usual calm and cold voice, "you to return immediately, Nathaniel. Your chores need to be done."

He doesn't wait for a response and turns to head back into the church. I see Father Mat rush from the church with a flashlight and begin helping people while Jude just ignores everything and disappears into the church.

Nate watches him go, then hugs Kira to him to help her calm down.

"Are you ok?" he asks her.

Kira nods, leaning into his shoulder, and snuggling closer when he keeps his arm around her.

Nate smiles and I can't help smiling myself. However, even as he smiles, he is glancing around the darkened yard and the people still recovering from the strange light show.

"Kira," he asks quietly, "would your parents mind if you were a little late because we helped out here?"

She shakes her head and replies quietly, "no, they wouldn't mind. You're such a good guy, Nate. Thanks."

He nods and hugs her closer as they walk across the yard to help. The smile on his face threatening to split his cheeks as they walk together.

"Hey Mr. Sornson, can we help?"

Mr. Sornson, one of the many neighbours within Little Haven, smiles in gratitude to the young couple.

Nate and Kira help out and I can't help but say, [*good boy.*]

He pauses and shoots me a content smile.

❖ 5 ❖

The fall is still early, but with Little Haven being so close to the mountains there is a biting chill to the air and a light layer of snow already on the ground. The moon is up, full and beaming down on the community. It's also beaming down on two figures just inside the hedge maze behind the church, snuggled oh-so-very-close to one another. After a long moment, they part long enough to take a breath and one of them giggles quietly. I keep well back, giving Nate and Kira their privacy. I also keep an eye on the back of the church, a watch-out to make sure Mr. Jude or Kira's parents don't catch the kids skipping tonight's service to make out in the hedge maze.

Any plans I had of getting Nate out of here are long gone, now that he has Kira. I sigh, but truthfully, it's barely a sigh. Things are better, even Jude has backed off from making Nate's life miserable. Surprising really, after that night I had expected Nate to be in so much trouble, but Jude has been keeping himself out of Nate's way.

"Nate, are you sure we won't be caught?"

I keep my eyes on the church.

"Of course not," he replies, very sure of himself and in the secret that is me.

The windows, lit from within the church, are bright in the darkness of the backyard. I still wonder about the backyard lights and what happened. Jude has not changed them. I can't help but smile, hoping Jude is afraid of the lights, afraid of what happened to them, and maybe even afraid of Nate.

Kira glances through me towards the back of the church, not as confident as Nate that they are safe.

"But," she says, worry working its way into her voice now, "shouldn't we be with everyone else? It sounded like it was a very important service. Mom and Dad were really worked up about it."

Nate follows her gaze, but sees me in the way. I wave cheerfully. He just frowns.

[*Do not frown at me. I am not interrupting your spit swapping session.*]

[No, but you're not helping either.]

[*Fine, I will go look in on the service and see what everyone is up to. Ok?*]

Nate nods, to both me and Kira.

He says quietly to her, "We'll sneak back in a few minutes, ok?"

I don't see how she responds, I'm already on my way across the yard to the church, but I can hear them both sucking face again so I guess she is agreeable.

[*Do not forget to let her breath, my friend.*]

[Don't forget to shut up, Chaid,] is his response. I sigh again. Being intangible sucks.

I am half way across the yard when I hear something from the church. I stop, not sure what it was that I heard, but thinking it sounded like a faint scream from within. Now I hear nothing, but am uncomfortable. I'm sure it sounded like a scream. I start forward once more, this time slowly, quietly, and concentrating on listening to the church, then I stop again. I don't hear anything from the church, nothing at all. No choir, no sermons, no music, no chatter of a service finished. Silence.

[*Nate, something is wrong.*]

[Chaid, just go check that it's safe to sneak back in.]

[*No, Nate. I am serious...*]

I don't get a chance to finish, as some unseen force hits me like a tornado. I stumble to my knees, unable to move or think as it sweeps me into a vortex of nothingness. I am in shadow, darkness, and the sudden loss of everything around me. It's all being drained away; the light, the cold, the air, the sound, the life and breath of everyone in the community, and the souls of over three hundred residents. This unnatural vortex, unseeable and inescapable, sucks everything away and I am just barely holding on.

[*NATHANIEL!*]

I don't know if he hears me, if he can see me, if he can feel what I am feeling coming from the church, or if he is even still alive.

[*NATHANIEL, RUN, GET AWAY, SAVE YOURSELF!*]

I keep screaming for as long as I can, struggling to hold on against the soul shredding force of this vortex of nothingness.

I am lost. Darkness closes in.

❖ 6 ❖

I lurch to my feet, taking a ragged breath and preparing to use it to scream, but stop. The church is gone, the backyard is gone, the buildings and streets of Little Haven are gone, even the stupid hedge maze is gone.

I am standing in a featureless grey wasteland of ash that stretches as far as the eye can see. Everything is still and silent, and I am more frightened that I remember ever being before.

A sudden roar snaps my head up to see dark clouds swirling above my head. The roar sounds like hundreds of people screaming in super-slow motion terror, like a horror movie playing at a fraction of normal speed. It also sounds like the clouds are growling, and hungry. I can feel it, an insatiable hunger. No, it's this place that feels hungry. As the clouds twist and roil faster, I can feel the anticipation of the hunger beneath the ash; about to be fed.

I run, turning and sprinting out into the ash, leaving the only footprints to be seen within the vast expanse of wasteland. Behind me I can hear the roar intensify, and glancing up above me I can see the clouds churn into a twister reaching down towards me. I run faster.

The twister slams down into the ground behind me, exploding ash into the air and sending me flying. I turn, watching the twister funnel down into the ground. The screaming within the twister intensifies, and the ground rumbles. Hearing that sound, I can't help but imagine some feline monstrosity purring in pleasure.

I stand, slowly and careful not to let the winds whipping by catch hold of me. As the clouds churn into the ground, I see what is beneath the ash. Nothing. Darkness. Abyss. Emptiness. Endless hunger.

I want to tear my eyes away, yet find myself unable to look away.

The last thing I see is a collection of thick strands of that inky, empty darkness escape the hole in the ground. The strands of darkness whip around me, through the air and the last bit of rolling clouds. Then everything explodes into grey ash.

I am lost. Darkness closes in.

❖ 7 ❖

I lurch to my feet, taking a ragged breath and preparing to use it to scream, but stop. Someone else is already screaming. The back door of the church is open and two sets of frantic footprints in the snow lead from the open doorway and around the side of the church towards the front. Within the open doorway is the sprawled out and unmoving body of one of the residents of Little Haven. I recognize the body as Kira's mother, her eyes open wide and glazed over in death. It is horrible, she has a smile on her face.

Kira is the one screaming.

I turn to find Nate and Kira still by the entrance to the hedge maze. Kira is on her knees, still taking deep breaths and releasing them as horror stricken screams. Nate holds her, rocking her quietly, unable to do anything else.

[*Nate, what happened?*]

He looks up, slowly, unbelieving and perhaps still in shock.

[Chaid, what happened to you?]

I rush over to them both, doing my best to not let Kira's screaming overwhelm me. I kneel down next to them.

[*I do not know, my friend, I was gone. Nate... Nate!*]

He snaps his head away from the open church door, his eyes unfocused for a moment before finally seeing me.

[*Nate, tell me what happened, please.*]

He nods, collecting himself together. [You were gone and there was screaming in the church. I didn't know what to do, I kept Kira from running in the church cause I didn't know what was happening and you were gone. You were gone!]

He is starting to lose it again, so I lean closer and say in a calm, quiet voice, [*shhhhhhh, Nate. I am very sorry I was gone, but I will not be disappearing again. Now, please tell me what happened next?*]

It takes him a moment, but he calms back down and continues, [well, the screaming stopped and it was quiet. For a long time it was quiet. Then the door opened and Father Mat stumbled out into the snow. He ran around the side of the church and was gone.]

[*What about Mr. Jude?*]

[Mr. Jude,] he says, then stops and begins to tremble. I don't know if he's going to be able to go on or not when suddenly he continues. [Yes, he came out behind Father Mat. I called out to him and he paused to look at me. That is when I noticed the knife in his hand. It... Chaid, it had blood all over it.]

[*What did he do then?*]

Fresh tears are falling down Nate's face.

[He smiled at me, just smirked. He pointed the knife at me and Kira, then went running after Father Mat. After he was gone we noticed her. She's dead, she's... just dead...]

He trails off and sits there, trembling and crying, while Kira continues her screaming. Her voice is getting hoarse and slowly the screams begin to fail until she is quiet.

I don't know what to do, except let them try to recover, so I rise and turn away from them both. I look at the church. I don't want to go in there, but I don't know what else to do. I need to figure out what is going on if I am going to help Nate survive this.

I head towards the church. I half expect Nate to notice me leaving and call me back. I realize that I am hoping Nate tells me not to leave them. He doesn't though, so I head into the church.

The bodies are everywhere. The pews are full, everyone in Little Haven was in attendance and now they are all gone. Whatever Jude did to them, and I have no doubt in my mind that it was Jude who did this, hit them quick and suddenly. They died almost instantly and without pain. It seems like it should be a good thing that there was no pain, but the smiles and looks of happiness and surprise on everyone's faces send constant shivers all along my spine and I want nothing more than to get out of there. Almost nothing more. I want Nate to get out of this alive more than anything.

Not everyone died so sudden and painlessly. I find a couple residents of the community downstairs, covered in blood. Pain, terror, shock, and surprise are on their faces. Everyone trusted Jude, now they are all dead. Threats and promises of revenge die on my lips before I can speak them. It would be difficult to fulfill such promises when you're nothing more than an observer. Jude should pay though.

I make sure I haven't missed anyone still alive and in need of help, but only find death. I head back upstairs to leave the church and check on Nate and Kira. I am almost outside of the church when I stop, suddenly very afraid. I can feel that hunger again, here in the church, right now. I don't know what that place was, but that same eternal hunger from beneath the ash is seeping into the church.

I notice then that the front door is now open. I am pretty sure it was closed before, and I am almost sure that Mr. Sornson's dead body was sprawled out in the aisle next to it. I don't see his body anywhere now. I look frantically around, desperate to find it, desperate to find out that it's not really missing. I search until the growing sense of that hunger becomes too terrifying for me to stay any longer and I flee the church.

[*Nate, we have to go, now.*]

I call out to him. He is huddled in the cold with the now exhausted Kira. In response, he looks up at me, his eyes struggling to focus.

[*We have to get help before he comes back to kill you and Kira, come on!*]

He rises, pulling Kira up with him. She

struggles, weakly, but Nate has no problem pulling her along. I lead, heading into the street will be the fastest way to get home, to grab enough stuff, to get out of Little Haven, and to survive.

Nate follows without saying anything, not questioning where we are going or why, just following. Kira barely seems aware of anything, allowing Nate to pull her along.

As we are walking around the corner of the church to leave the backyard she suddenly whimpers. Turning her head to look behind us at the rear entrance of the church, her eyes widening in shock and a mixture of hope and terror.

In her oh-so-quiet voice, she says, "mom?"

[*Do not stop, Nate, keep moving!*]

We keep going. I don't want to go back to find out what Kira saw. I don't even want to think about what she might have seen. I move faster, trying to get us all away from the church. Nate follows, pulling Kira along with him even though she is looking behind us, and crying again. I am so very glad that he trusts me enough to follow my lead without hesitation or questioning. Either, I feel, could cost us our lives this night.

We get across the street and into the house.

❖ 8 ❖

I go first, because that only makes sense. The front door is open. Nate shovelled the walk earlier so I can't see any fresh footprints in the snow to know if Mat and Jude are in there... or something worse. I step into the darkness of the house and pause there. I listen and am glad I don't have to breathe because I am sure my terrified breathing would be the only thing I could hear.

I hear nothing, the house is quiet. It feels empty, or I could just be hoping it is so. Nothing seems out of place and I look around the main floor. I find nobody here.

[*Nate, the downstairs is clear, bring Kira in. We have to be quick if we want to get out of here.*]

I hear the two of them enter the house and close the door behind them. Nate picks up the nearest phone and frowns.

"The phone line is dead," he says.

No phones, crap.

[Chaid, what do we do?]

[*Warm clothes for travelling, some food and water. Backpacks to carry it all. Flashlights. Can you find this all here?*]

He nods to me, setting Kira down into a chair and covering her with a small, but warm couch blanket. He rummages around in the kitchen, starting to gather supplies. I head upstairs to make sure the house is really empty. I search through the rooms and find no one.

[Chaid, can I come upstairs?]

[*Yes, the house is empty.*]

Nate moves quickly upstairs and gathers the last of the supplies. I am about to head back downstairs when I catch a glimpse through a window of movement outside. I turn to the window and lean forward to look out over the community. I can't see anything now, but the hedge maze is very dark. There could be people moving through it, shifting shadows that could also just be my frightened imagination playing tricks on me. I look across the compound to the far side and the single gate that leads through the wall and out of Little Haven. One small guard house is stationed there, its lights on as it is always manned. That is where we need to get.

My musings are interrupted by a sudden high pitched scream from downstairs -Kira- that is just as suddenly cut short. The silence in the aftermath of the terrified scream freezes me in place. Both the silence and my inaction are broken a moment later as Nate charges downstairs.

"Kira!," he yells.

I follow right behind him, hoping against all hope that she is ok.

She isn't.

Jude has her in the living room, sitting next to him on the couch. A sadistic grin on his face and a bloody knife in his hand, which he is holding calmly against her throat. A quick glance down the hall shows me the open door to the garage and I can't believe how stupid I was to not have checked the garage.

"Good evening, Nathaniel," he says in that cool, calm voice of his. Makes me feel like razor-sharp icicles are being pressed into the flesh under my fingernails.

"You skipped out of tonight's sermon," he says, pausing to click his tongue at Nate, "that was very bad of you."

The knife presses close, leaving a smear of thick

blood on her neck from the knife. The malicious grin on Jude's face grows wider. "Very bad of you both."

Nate is frozen in terror, unable to do anything to help Kira or himself. I am frozen as well, powerless to do anything.

Jude's eyes shift back to Nate. "And what do you think would be a fitting punishment for you two bad children? Nathaniel?"

As bad as that question was before, it is now infinitely more cruel and tormenting. Nate begins to tremble in helpless terror. He opens his mouth to try to speak, but the only thing that comes out is a squeak that sort of sounds like he is trying to say, "no, please..."

Jude laughs, sudden and shocking, then stops just as abruptly and points the knife at Nate.

Angrily he yells at Nate, "Nathaniel! You know bad boys are punished, and you have been very, very bad! Now choose your punishment!"

"No," whispers Nate.

Jude stops his rant, looks at Nate and leans forward which causes Kira to whimper. Roughly clamping his free hand over her mouth, he shushes her and then looks back at Nate. Nate has his hands clenched into shaking fists at his side and is leaning forward a bit towards Jude.

"Speak up, Nathaniel!"

Nate closes his eyes then and leans forward a bit more, looking like he is about to fall forward on his face.

"No," Nate whispers again, this time through tightly clenched teeth.

"What," yells Jude, "shall I choose your punishment then?"

Nate's eyes flicker open then, staring straight at Jude. His hands open and he flings his arms wide, even as he leans forward even more. It is impossible that he is not falling, yet he remains up on the tips of his toes. Nate does all this at the same time as he screams at the top of his lungs, "NOOOOOOOOO!"

Every lightbulb in the house blows in a simultaneous shower of sparks. Blue-white and blinding surges of electricity arc from one wall outlet to another all over the house.

"NOOOOOOOOOOOOOOOOOO!"

Nate continues to scream. One arc of electricity shoots across the room and almost hits Jude. The former foster father launches himself backwards away from the deadly lightning, his eyes wide. Kira falls forward to sprawl on the floor. She scrambles away from the couch and Jude, towards Nate.

Jude stands up, his eyes still wide, but now blinded by the arcs of electricity. Suddenly Nate rocks back, resting fully on his feet, and his agonizing scream stops. The arcs of electricity flash out of existence, plunging the house back into darkness. Jude blinks, trying to work the haze out of his eyes so he can see again. That blood-stained knife is still clenched in his hand.

"Nathaniel," Jude says in the quiet menace he has always terrorized Nate with.

"No," responds Nate quietly, cutting off whatever Jude was about to say, and every outlet in the living room surges again with electricity. Half a dozen bolts of blue-white lightning arc into Jude. It lasts a long moment, Nate calmly watching with nothing showing in his eyes as Jude is electrocuted. Finally it stops, the lightning blinks out of existence, and a scorched and unrecognizable Jude falls to the ground dead.

Nate just stands there, arms and hands hanging limply by his sides, staring at the smoking charred corpse that used to be his guardian. A liar, a sadistic tormentor, a betrayer, and a murderer. Now, just dead.

[*Nate?,*] I ask tentatively, after a moment of silence.

"No," he responds quietly, still staring at the body. "No, and never again."

I leave him to recover and walk over to the windows. Outside the community of Little Haven is in complete darkness. The electricity is completely blown over the entire community. I replay Nate's outburst and wonder how much power Nate has built up within him, if he just unloaded it through years of pent up rage and pain, or if it has just laid more onto his shoulders.

I glance back and am relieved to see Kira up off the floor with her arms around Nate. She has pulled him out of the living room and into the kitchen, away from the body. She is stronger of spirit than I thought, and I am glad for Nate's sake. I turn back to the window and watch the darkness of the streets in the night, giving them time and space to find some semblance of recovery.

❖ 9 ❖

I don't know how much time has passed, but I wait patiently, letting the two kids try to recover from the night's horrors. I just wish I could say that the horrors were over. I strongly doubt it.

A flash of light from outside the house grabs my attention, a stab of spotlight flashing down from the sky above Little Haven. It's a helicopter. I run upstairs to a better window.

[*Nate, get up here, and don't leave Kira alone.*]

He races upstairs, still not questioning me, with Kira in tow. By the time they make it to the bedroom window we can all hear the sound of the chopper's engines. Unfortunately they don't sound healthy. The spotlight is turning in circles, the helicopter spinning above the community.

"Nate, who are they?" Kira quietly asks.

Nate gathers Kira closer to him as he shakes his head and watches the out of control helicopter that has mysteriously appeared above Little Haven.

"I don't know," he says in a tired and worn voice, "but it can't be a coincidence that they have appeared here tonight."

I turn, catch his eye, and nod in agreement.

"We should avoid them, they could have been working with... Jude."

He cringes as he speaks Jude's name. Kira cringes too, and I probably cringe a bit myself. I can't blame any of us.

All three of us turn back to the window as the spinning light starts spiralling across the community more and more out of control. The helicopter's engine starts coughing, struggling to keep the vehicle aloft. After a valiant struggle, it fails and the aircraft spirals downward to crash in the middle of the community. Dead centre of the hedge maze. Fireballs explode from the crash and Kira just manages to keep a scream quieted down to a whimper.

[*We need to get out of here.*]

Nate nods and says quietly to Kira, "we need to get out of here," and pulls her away from the window.

I go ahead of them, check out the downstairs again and decide to go check the garage while Nate grabs everything he was packing before.

[*Nate, do not bring Kira into the garage.*]

[Almost ready to go,] he responds, not asking me why I don't want him in the garage. I am glad. He doesn't need to see anymore carnage. I guess Father Mat really was just a good guy, a priest who cared for this community. He wasn't evil like Jude. Didn't save him though, poor guy.

I go back to Nate and Kira. They are just about ready, packing away food and water. I notice them avoiding the living room and am not surprised. I have no desire to go anywhere near there either.

We are ready, gathered by the back door. With Kira held close, Nate takes a deep breath and opens the door to the darkness. We step out and are gone.

❖ 10 ❖

I go first, because -again- that only makes sense. Without the power, the entire community is in darkness, but the full moon helps. I peek around the front of the house and immediately regret it. There are... shadows... in the street, lumbering around in some sort of confused shamble. It's like some horrible zombie movie. I shudder then, because that might not be so far off of the mark.

We head into the hedge maze instead. Every backyard has an entrance and I have gotten to know the maze fairly well recently. Nate and Kira are not happy about entering the maze, but Nate is still following my lead and so far we have survived. So far.

It's quiet as we move through the maze, steadily moving towards the front gate and, hopefully, safety. The occasional gust of chill wind gusts over the outer wall and sweeps across the hedge maze, setting the hedges rustling lightly. That, and the soft crush of snow under winter boots, is all I can hear. Then I hear something else.

[*Nate, quiet.*]

I stop and wave behind me for Nate to stop and crouch down while I listen. The wind settles, the sound of our footsteps disappear, but I can still hear slow shuffling footsteps moving through the hedges nearby.

[What is it?]

[*Someone is in the maze with us. Just stay put, stay quiet. I will investigate.*]

I hear the soft whispering of Nate calming Kira down behind me. They both fall quiet and I can hear those shuffling footsteps again in the silence.

I move forward, not having to worry about making any noise, and try to track the sound of footsteps to see who it is. I peek around the corner of a hedge and see a shadow shuffling through the maze not too far away. It turns around the corner of the maze and is disappearing down another path so I step out to better see who it is. That is when it stops and turns back towards me. I freeze. Can it see me? I rush back to cover, behind the corner of the hedge, and hear it begin moving again. Now it is moving towards me and it is moving faster. Who is this? What is going on?

I run back to Nate and Kira who are still huddled together.

[*Nate, someone is coming, we have to hide.*]

Nate pulls Kira up with him and follows me. They are being as quiet as they can, but we can still hear the shuffling footsteps moving faster and closer to us. I pull us around several turns and bends in the maze, putting as many of the confusing maze-ways between us and our pursuer as I can.

We turn a corner and almost run into a dead end. I have taken a wrong turn somewhere and now we are trapped. The shuffler is not too far away, getting closer. I hunker down and motion for Nate to do the same. Nate and Kira huddle together, staying quiet. The only thing we can hear now is the dragging footsteps of whoever is hunting us, getting closer and closer.

As the footsteps shuffle by us, just on the other side of the hedge we are huddling behind, Kira muffles a whimper in the puffy sleeve of her winter coat. The footsteps pause and even I try to hold my breath.

[*Whatever you do Nate, do not move or make a sound.*]

It turns then, shuffling a step or two back towards us, until it is directly beside us on the other side of the hedge. Nate hugs Kira closer to him, and I notice she has her eyes squeezed closed and is burying most of her face in Nate's shoulder.

It turns towards us, now facing us on the other side of the hedge, and I realize that it makes absolutely no noise other than the sound of its footprints in the snow. I can't hear it breathing, can't hear the swish of its arms swinging in a winter coat as it walks, can't hear it fiddle with something in the dark or even make a misstep or brush against the hedge. It is completely silent.

I close my eyes, huddle down, and think or hope or pray that if we make absolutely no noise and remain absolutely still, it will leave us alone. I think it over and over in my mind; leave us alone, go away, leave and find someone else to bother, just get out of here, we are not here, nothing is here, please just leave, please...

[Chaid?]

I open my eyes, the continuous looping thoughts going through my mind cut off, and find us still here.

[*Yes Nate?*]

[They're gone.]

I can hear faint shuffling steps moving farther away from us in the maze. I don't actually breathe, but if I did, I would be breathing a big sigh of relief. I still take a moment to collect myself.

[*Ok, good. Let us go. We are not far from the guard house at the front gate.*]

❖ 11 ❖

The guard house is another dead end. We reach the edge of the maze and sneak through the last house's yard to the front gate to find it closed and securely locked. There is an intercom on the wall next to the gate, but no one answers. We are now in the backyard of that last house again, where I can feel more secure being near so many hiding places.

[Chaid, what do we do now?]

Kira looks up at Nate and whispers, "what do we do now Nate?"

Both of them sound on the verge of tears and I myself wonder just what we can do now.

Nate answers Kira before I can think of a reply for him. "We need to get out of Little Haven, that hasn't changed, but we need to get through that gate."

[*And we need a vehicle of some kind,*] I add.

"And we need a vehicle in case the guards are all gone too," he finishes.

Kira grabs Nate's arm and begins to pull him back toward the house. She whispers to him, "Nate, all the vehicles have a trigger for the gate. We can take any of them."

And she is right, and I feel so stupid making us sneak around the maze for the past hour or so. We just need to grab a car and drive out of here. I rush to catch up to them, feeling just a touch of hope.

We don't have to break into the garage. With such an open, trusting, secure community, who would even feel the need to lock things up? Finding the keys is a little more difficult. I go first and I check everything in the house before I let Nate and Kira come in. Kira has yet to ask Nate how he can tell when it is safe to enter. But with all the strangeness of the night, it's not really all that surprising. Regardless, she waits quietly with Nate until I give the all clear. We find the keys and head back to the car in the garage.

The car starts up and -we are in luck- the garage door is not automatic, so Nate gets it open without any difficulty. Nate sits in the driver's seat, his long legs able to reach the pedals and still let him see just over the dash. Nate tentatively pulls out of the garage and slowly drives out into the empty street and turns towards the community gate.

We are getting out of here. We are going to make it. I think this, I feel it, I may even have a bit of a smile on my face. Then Kira gasps, opens her door and jumps out of the very slow moving car.

"Kira!," Nate yells, struggling to stop the car and put it into park. He finally manages, and opens his door to chase after her.

[*Nate, stop.*]

I say it, but would not be surprised if he ignored me for the first time tonight. He does pause to study the street Kira is running down. It was empty a few minutes ago, but not any longer.

Several shadows are shuffling down the moonlit street towards us. Kira is running straight for one of them and I can make out just enough detail to recognize Kira's mother. The last time I saw this woman, she was dead. Now she is holding her arms out towards Kira.

"KIRA!"

Nate shouts again, and takes a step away from

the car, but I stop him again.

[*Nate, that is not Kira's mother. Her mother is dead. I saw her, dead...*]

Nate scowls, and cuts me off by running past me towards Kira. I don't blame him, not really. I follow to try to make sure he doesn't die.

Nate is sprinting, calling out Kira's name. He is fast, pulling far ahead of me.

Kira has stopped just out of reach of her mother and I hear the girl say in that quiet voice of hers, "mom?"

She sounds confused and scared again. I know Nate hears it too because he is running even faster.

Kira's mother gathers the little girl in her arms and we both hear Kira whimper. We are close enough to make out Kira's mother more clearly and I stop dead as I realize she has no eyes. Not empty sockets or anything gruesome like that, just pools of thick darkness where her eyes should be. I know I have seen that darkness before, beneath the ash of that strange wasteland.

It's a hungry darkness, eternally hungry.

Tendrils of that darkness slip forth. This causes even Nate to stop in horror. We hear Kira whisper quietly, "mom?" one last time before those tendrils strike.

"NOOOOOOOOOOO!" Nate screams as the tendrils of darkness spear through Kira's eyes and into her. She jerks once before starting to collapse, but her mother holds her tightly. The darkness continues to pour forth and into the little girl. Kira's mouth is open and something very dark and very thick dribbles out of it and down her chin. I don't know if it is blood or more of that darkness. Looking around, I see that more... things are shuffling closer. I have to get Nate out of here, now.

[*NATE! We have to get out of here before they get you too!*]

Nate starts back towards me, but stops almost immediately. I turn around to see that we are now surrounded by them. Each and every one is a former resident of Little Haven, and I know they all died in the church tonight. I see no eyes in any of them, just those pools of hungry shadow. They reach out towards us, making no noise. Nate moves to my side, not knowing what to do and I don't know what to say if he asks. He doesn't ask, and I see tears glitter in the moonlight as they slide down his face.

The things move in, surrounding us. As they get closer the darkness pours out of their eyes into halos of writhing dark tendrils.

I feel the hunger, such hunger. A hunger that could never be sated.

[Chaid, are we going to die?]

He is strangely calm, or perhaps so beyond terrified that he just seems calm.

[*I am so very sorry, my friend. It was very good to know you Nate. You are a good friend.*]

A smaller figure moves in front of the others, faster than them or just more hungry. It is Kira, dead like the rest, and her face also surrounded by a trembling mass of dark tendrils sprouting from her empty eyes. She rushes towards Nate.

Nate falls to his knees as Kira reaches out to

embrace him. I close my eyes, fearing this is the end, but nothing happens. I hear Kira whisper, "Nate, please."

My eyes snap open in disbelief. Kira is standing just out of reach of Nate, her arms wrapped tightly around herself. She is just barely holding herself back. The hungry tendrils of darkness are whipping around her head in agitation and she is trembling with the effort to keep from launching herself at Nate.

She opens her mouth to speak again, and I can see more of the darkness starting to snake its way out of her mouth. She still manages, in a quiet voice full of desperation and pain, to whisper again, "Nate. Please!"

[*Nate!*]

He screams.

It's not even discernible as a word this time, just pure primal rage and anguish being released. His eyes blaze orange red like they are on fire and then an inferno of actual flame explodes forth from him. The flames blast outward, rocking the darkness-possessed dead away from him, and then enveloping them in the flames. They make no sound as they are incinerated.

I lose sight of everything but fiery destruction. I can still hear Nate screaming over the roar of the flames as the fiery destruction spreads further and further across Little Haven.

I am lost. Darkness closes in.

- Chapter 7: Unknown -

"At any moment something new could be discovered, something that could make everything known about the universe obsolete. Real wisdom is knowing that nothing can ever be really, fully known. Unfortunately, this can be a bitter truth to swallow. Sometimes it can kill."   – *unknown*

I am unknown.
I am a shadow.
I am a liar,
And I am the lie.
I am the seventh,
I am the last.
This is not my story,
My story is not for you to know.

- Epilogue -

"When one stares into the abyss, it is not the abyss that stares back, but one's own reflection that glares defiantly out of that dark." *– unknown*

"You are angry, I know this."

His voice is the rumble of thunder after lightning strikes the ground where you are standing, leaving you deaf and stunned.

"I know you, and what I know is acceptable. But of that which I do not know, that is entirely different."

His voice is the subsonic rumble of colliding continents and the sudden upheaval of the earth in a civilization ending earthquake.

"It is not acceptable, this not knowing. So, to rectify this unknowing do tell me then of what became of them after the incident. This, I must know."

The silence that follows is the cold, absolute quiet of the abyss between the stars. It lasts for exactly as long as He wills it to, which seems to be forever.

"You will answer my questions, servant."

I cannot speak, as I have no mouth, but it is not necessary. I answer, as I must, and He hears me.

[*They were separated, kept apart.*]

I try to open my eyes, but it is difficult to summon the strength through the ceaseless pain of my existence. Difficult, but not impossible. I am angry, am nothing else, really, but endless anger. I let it build up, even welcome it, and it bursts through the pain. Giving me the strength to open my eyes.

I see the hard packed, grey ash that I am kneeling upon, have been kneeling upon since time began and perhaps even before then. I see the grey spread out around me, endless; the featureless wastelands of ash.

I see the two sets of chains that bind me, pooling around me in the dust. Bound to my left, chains the darkest of black void, a burning frost that has long turned the flesh they bind to a frozen, lifeless white. Bound to my right, chains the fluid crimson of liquid fire, scorching flesh to a dark and cracked char, down to the bone.

"YOU FACILITATED THIS SEPARATION, BY YOUR DESIGN?"

My eyes snap closed, my full attention and focus demanded by the force of His will.

[*No.*]

My will splinters into infinite shards, broken by agony. An eternity later, He allows me to restore my mind, returning so I might answer once again.

[*I might have, though I did not do so consciously. I was, however, pleased by their separation.*]

"THIS IS TRUE, I KNOW, BUT DO NOT KNOW THE ANSWER TO THE QUESTION OF WHY? IN WHAT WAY DID THEIR SEPARATION SERVE YOUR PURPOSE?"

[*I serve, in all things, only you.*]

Agony, again and for an unknowably long time. Then nothingness for even longer, until he draws me back.

"DO NOT PANDER EMPTY WORDS, DEVOID OF

MEANING, TO ME, SERVANT."

I do not answer, knowing that any answer will only serve to summon more pain. I try to open my eyes once more, but even my significant rage abandons me in the wake of His punishments.

He continues.

"I KNOW YOU SERVE ME, IN ALL THINGS. THAT YOU DO NOT ACCEPT THIS TO BE TRUE IS, IN NO WAY, NECESSARY FOR ITS CONTINUANCE TO BE THE TRUTH. SO SAVE YOUR WORTHLESS PRATTLE AND GIVE UNTO ME THAT WHICH HAS BEEN RIGHTFULLY DEMANDED."

I would remain silent, but must answer.

[*I wished for them to be on their own. To grow up without guidance or manipulations. I wished for them to simply be themselves.*]

Silence. Worlds could be born and destroyed in the gravity of that silence.

"THAT YOU BELIEVE THEY WOULD BE FREE OF OUR MANIPULATIONS IS AN ABSURDITY."

[*I did only speak the...*]

"OH YOU SPEAK TRUTH, INDEED. I KNOW THIS, BUT I KNOW TOO THAT YOU HIDE A DEEPER TRUTH BEHIND YOUR FAITHFUL ANSWER."

I try to open my eyes once more, urging on the anger and rage. I feel it flow, a mere trickle makes it through the trauma of his punishments and dominance, but enough. I open my eyes once more to the forever greyness of the wastelands of ash. It is a comfort to me, my only comfort. It lasts for only a moment before He demands my attention once again, and my eyes close.

"DO NOT BE CONCERNED, YOU HAVE ANSWERED

TRUE ENOUGH. I KNOW. I KNOW YOU, AS I KNOW YOUR VERY ESSENCE. YOU SHOULD ACCEPT THIS, FOR ARE YOU NOT THE SON OF MY WILL?"

[*Yes...*]

I try. I try everything I can, but all the rage in all of existence does but falter against His will and I must call him, [*... Father.*]

"I KNOW, SERVANT, I KNOW YOU HATE. WOULD IT PLEASE YOU TO KNOW THAT YOUR HATE IS ACCEPTABLE? YOUR HATE IS PERMITTED, SO CONTINUE TO HARBOR IT AS YOU WILL. AS YOU SERVE ME IN ALL THINGS, YOU WILL CONTINUE TO SERVE ME, EVEN IN YOUR HATE. I KNOW THIS, THUS SHALL IT BE TRUTH."

I say and think nothing about this, for it is no revelation to me. I was created from His will and power, so even my hate comes from Him as just another part of my design.

"ONE LAST QUESTION, THEN SHALL I LEAVE YOU TO YOUR DUTIES, SERVANT."

[*Yes?*]

"AS THE OTHERS WERE HUNTED, ARE THESE TOO HUNTED?"

[*They are, by many -both mortal and immortal- who would use and destroy them.*]

"YES, MANY. THE ATTENTIONS OF THE DANGEROUS AND WICKED ARE DRAWN TO THEM, FOR THAT IS THEIR PURPOSE. BUILT INTO THEIR VERY DESIGN, THIS IS, TO BAIT OUR NEMESIA. KNOWN TO BOTH YOU AND I, THIS IS, AND SO YOU DO NOT ANSWER WHAT I AM TRULY ASKING OF YOU, SERVANT."

Once more into pain does he banish me. I should regret my insolence, but I do not. It is the only pleasure to be gained for someone such as myself.

"You know of what and who I speak of, but just to be clear, I shall reform the question. Has their separation served to hinder her efforts or has your meddling only served to make it easier for her to hunt them?"

[*She; exiled of the wretched wastes, the woeful witchbite of innocence-in-nightmare, the fallen, the wingless, the betrayed and betrayer...*] I go all old-old-old-school in the titles, simultaneously making sure He knows that I am answering the damn question and dragging out my answer to take one more small dig at Him. [*...nameless, but once known as Wiieth ob'Zuthiel does hunt them still, but has yet to make any move against any of them or attempt to draw them together. Her plans, if any, remain hidden from me.*]

He weighs the worth of my answer, possibly contemplating if any further punishment is deserved, then replies.

"We shall watch and see, and take measures accordingly. For now, gather them together, servant."

[*It has already begun.*]

"Good."

His voice fades and in its place does stillness reign. Stillness and the continued pain from the chains that shackle me. I endure it, for it is nothing I have not already endured for an eternity or two.

Eventually I will have to return to them, even though I do not wish to. It is true, I do hate. The source of my rage and only power I have. Hate; for them, for Him, for all Creation, and most of all for myself. I summon my anger, embrace it and open my eyes to watch the wastelands of ash, as much as I can before I have to go back to them.

I wonder how better Creation would be without it all. To have nothingness, and the peace such absence would bring. Would this peace be better? I have studied nothingness, for it is all I see in the ashlands.

I decide that I find it to be quite lovely.

This is only the beginning...

The journey of Seven Crows continues in Book II of the Seven Crows series, by Justin Killam. Or create your own tales with your own set of Seven Crow characters, within the Seven Crows world, with the pen & paper Role Playing Game. Stay tuned to the 7crows website or like J.Killam Writer on Facebook for more information and updates.

7crows.huntandkillam.ca

Justin Killam:
Gamer, Writer, Philosopher, Publisher, Teacher, Novelist, Theologian, Author, Game Designer, and...

A storyteller all of his life, Justin first got into weaving tales of the fantastic while playing classic pen and paper RPGs like D&D, VtM, and his own home brewed awesomeness. Creating stories interactively with a group of friends, spending hours obsessing over every facet of a character and their development, makes character driven stories an absolute must. Combining storytelling with gaming is still a huge part of his life, when he can fit it into the busy schedule of being a husband and teacher in his home town of Yarmouth, Nova Scotia. Seven Crows is his first novel, set in a world that has been developing within his mind since studying Theology and Philosophy at STFX.

If you are a teacher, please email. I have been using this novel in my middle and high school ELA classes for several years and have many assignments that I would be happy to share.

APOC.HUNTANDKILLAM@GMAIL.COM

Call to Arms!
I need two things to become a successful indi-author!

I: An Epic Novel.
Seems like a no-brainer. If my novel is not worth telling your best friend about, then it's not going to matter how much time and effort I put into marketing, no one is going to care. Hopefully I have succeeded with this. Hopefully you have read my novel and can't wait for your best friend to read it so you two can argue over who the seventh crow really is, or why the limo was at the base of Bruknows Hill, or what the proper pronunciation is for Chaid's name. Hopefully you can't wait for the next novel. Well, there is most definitely going to be another novel, and the more successful this novel is, the sooner the next will be released. Which leads me to the second thing...

II: You.
Yes, you. I need you in order to be successful. Why? Well, cause your awesome! You bought my book and read it, right? Well, that is awesome! That is one person who has enjoyed my work! You tell a friend how awesome Seven Crows is and they buy it, which doubles to two people who have enjoyed my work! Now tell more friends, go to amazon and goodreads and post reviews, spreading the word even farther! If everyone you told about my book did the same thing, you buying and enjoying my work would become hundreds, if not thousands of people buying and enjoying my work! That is why I need you, because without you doing this, no one will know just how awesome Seven Crows is.

And thank you, for your support.
- Justin Killam

Conscience of a Blackened Street

A Seven Crows Short Story
by Justin Killam

❖ 1 ❖
Basement Apartment
Dr. Samuel Tynan's Free-Clinic
72 North Covenant Drive
The Dunes
12:28 am

The clinic is cold. The good doctor has as little concern for the cold as he does for the heat and generally manages to be completely ignorant of the temperature. As such, the pale, sweat-stained man sitting in the corner is blue-lipped and shivering with both the cold and shock.

The man on the operating table is not shivering. He's far too sedated for that. His breath plums out of a slack mouth, in vaporous gusts, and bare skin turned a shade beyond white.

Tynan's breath does not plume in the cold. Had the conscious man noticed this he might have thought twice about staying. As it is, he is thinking only about the score they just screwed up, the pain in his shattered elbow, and how he is going to explain all this to his boss. More or less in that order.

"Look, Doc, you can fix him up, right? I mean, he'll make it through, yeah? He's the boss's kid. I tell you that? His oldest son. It was supposed to be an easy score. In. Out. Cash on the barrelhead. But it all went bad. The others are dead. Scuffy. Minko. Ratter. All dead. Dead in the street. But I got em back. Got 'em good. Killed every one of those rat-faced-sons-a-bitches, and dragged the boss's kid here. It was just us got away. No one left to even see us go. Ah hell, the boss probably thinks we're dead too. And who's to tell him different?"

The street punk rambles on, panic gnawing away at his insides and setting his voice to a tremble. Tynan tunes him out, tunes everything out except the body before him with the bullet lodged in his lung. His focus, in its entirety, is upon the challenge that now lies before him and the opportunity it represents; life or death, with only Tynan standing upon the threshold between the two.

The good doctor checks his patient's pupil dilation and reflex response. The anesthetic is taking effect. The patent is almost ready.

❖ 2 ❖
A Street
The Dunes
4:20 am

The snow fall is thick, the large flakes of a gently falling white shroud. Like angel feathers from heaven. The good doctor stands unmoving in the middle of the street. The multi-shades of grey formal attire slowly turn white as snow layers him into a soft white statue. It is strangely luminous down the lane. Not from the few flickering streetlights that remain intact, or from the feeble light of half a dozen or so smeared and foggy windows along the lane. The brightness is coming from the snow; reflecting, refracting, redirecting what little light there is. The usual darkness of the filth and trash that pile across the sidewalks are being hidden away beneath the snow. It fills the lane with white brightness.

Above the good doctor a lamp flickers suddenly to life, spotlighting the unmoving figure. It seems as though he does not notice, but some deep part of his mind registers the street, the light, and the snow... some part.

"He that is slow to anger is better than the mighty and he who does rule his spirit shall receive..." Tynan blinks the thick layer of snow from his eyes and lifts his head. "Ahhh, the city, my garden... mine."

Snow falls from him, revealing the man beneath the snow. His grey suit isn't wet, as none of the snow melted. He blinks once more, unsure if he has just spoken aloud or if it was merely a thought within his mind. Unsure, but equally unconcerned. The wind picks up, blowing the rest of the snow from him and he steps through the sudden flurry and turns, leaving behind the street. Without worry he slips deeper into the darker alleys of the Dunes.

❖ 3 ❖

Basement Apartment
Dr. Samuel Tynan's Free-Clinic
72 North Covenant Drive
The Dunes
12:32 am

"I am skilled at what I do, my good man. Your friend can and will be saved, do not fall into despair on that account. I will insist, however, that you do indeed shut your abominable mouth before I end you."

Tynan speaks without any hint of anger or malice, just a smooth entrancing monotone. However, within that tone is the disturbing promise that what he speaks is undisputable truth.

With a gurgle the man with the busted up arm stills to silence. Overwhelmed by the cold, the shock, or some unknowable force flowing from the good doctor, the thug slumps to the floor with his eyes rolling back into his skull. He twitches every now and then, but being in no position to interfere with the operation, is ignored.

The good doctor looks over his patient, the splay of limbs, the slipping beyond pale body, the open bullet wound, the weakly pumping stream of blood from the ragged hole, the weak rattle of breath, crimson spittle wetting the little thief's lips. Mostly, what catches a moment of fascinated attention from Tynan is the utter helplessness of the victim. His victim? Something dark stirs and blossoms from deep within the twisted psyche of Tynan, something that hungers and pleads to be sated... as if it could ever.

With a hand that would be trembling if he were a lesser man, the good doctor deftly plucks from his assortment of tools and begins his work, delving into the flesh of the "boss's" son and begins his work. He is a skilled practitioner of the healing arts, and if this body should indeed expire, it shall be solely at the discretion of Tynan's will and nothing else...

NOTHING ELSE... nothing else...

❖ 4 ❖
An Alleyway
The Dunes
4:20 am

The twisted alleyways are narrow, walls of crumbling brick or rotting lumber fortified with layers of compressed trash. He follows the labyrinth of decay without hesitation, knowing his path and his destination. He arrives; a small cul-de-sac just off a crossroads of narrow lanes and cramped with overlooking buildings attempting to crowd out the minuscule cut of cloudy sky above. A small amount of snow flutters down from above, managing to slip into the alleyway and lightly coat the pavement. It does little to hide the splay of dead bodies. Thick splatters and rivulets of crimson contrast with the white snow in patterns like deep red blossoms and delicate petals of dead flesh. Tynan stares, entranced for a time.

He looks up, once again breaking the settling layer of snow into a scattering of white. Emerging from another alley is a heavy set man, dressed warmly in expensive brand label wear and wielding a hefty pistol in a shiny leather gloved hand. Dark, hard eyes stare out from within his hood. The good doctor says nothing, studying those eyes as the man cautiously approaches. The darkness within those eyes whispers of having witnessed petty and depraved things, and willed even more such things to be done. But now the hard and sharp core of darkness has softened with worry and pain. And Tynan is intrigued.

"Greetings... I assume you would be the boss I have heard so much relentless blather about?"

The man's pistol flashes up and into the good doctor's face, "you can give up the cash, the ice, and the Will-Born or you can give up your life extremely slowly."

The good doctor reacts in no way, but continues to stare into the man's eyes, answering in the drawn out calm of his monotone voice, "Will-Born? Ah, I see, you mean your son. You are concerned for him?"

A stream of curses and threats, lasting a full minute, is the good doctor's answer and displays the hood's only real concern, which is for his property and profit. Tynan listens a moment, pulling together the frayed strings of information gained from the angry man before him.

There is a touch of genuine disappointment in his unwavering voice as he speaks again. "A man's life consists not in the abundance of things which he possesses," he points to the bodies lying around them, "you would do well to consider this lesson, that which they have already learned, perhaps then it might not cost you so dear a price."

The "boss" opens his mouth to launch into what sounds like the beginning of another long tirade of threats and insults and simultaneously cocks back his gun wielding hand. The good doctor blinks a single time as he observes the increasing threat of imminent physical violence.

"Cease."

The man stops, instantly, in the middle of an unimaginative threat with a gurgle. There is a moment of stillness and silence. Then, hand trembling and eyes bulging, the man drops the pistol barrel back down towards the good doctor's face. Tynan observes, unmoving, while crimson twilight within floods his mind, hazes over his grey eyes, and a war of wills is waged against himself.

His will is set. But his will is set. It is...

❖ 5 ❖
Basement Apartment
Dr. Samuel Tynan's Free-Clinic
72 North Covenant Drive
The Dunes
1:35 am

Relaxed once more, the good doctor begins to perform. The battle raged between his will and the deep seated desires of the crimson twilight within has left no residual effect on the good doctor's focus, and he performs efficiently with considerable skill. The body on the table that hovers between this world and the next will be saved, should Tynan decide it is a life is worth saving.

He has not yet decided.

Flesh parts almost eagerly to the good doctor's scalpel, and the secrets contained within that flesh part just as easily to Tynan's all-too-aware mind, spilling forth a steaming pile of twisted thoughts and impressions. Delicate, like bundles of nerves and just as charged, Tynan sorts through them to glean the message of this one's soul. A message for him, or a test perhaps.

"Save... me..."

Tynan stops and leans back away from the body not yet stitched back together. He is unsure if the broken body before him had just spoken aloud or if it was merely a resonance of desire from an unconscious man. Once more Tynan is unaware and unconcerned of which might be the case, for either way is the message clear.

With revelation gleaned, the good doctor's decision is made and he leans close to the body to whisper in its ear, "he who asks truly, shall receive and as such, I tell you that today you will be with me and made whole once more."

The unconscious punk on the floor with the busted up arm is not so lucky.

The demands of the crimson twilight within must be sated.

❖ 6 ❖
An Alleyway
The Dunes
4:32 am

"Father!"

The gun wielding thug spins around and points his gun at the son stepping out of the shadows. Dressed in a simple thin wrapping of a hospital gown, he does not appear to feel the cold or notice his bare feet almost blue in the snow. He is still very much beyond pale and there is a feverish glint in his too-wide eyes.

"Will-Born, where's the ice...," the thug trails off, recognizing the strange garb his son is wearing.

"What the fu..."

Again he trails off, but not of his own choice this time. His son steps forward and slashes open the thug, his father. A wide clean gash cut from one side of his neck to the other with a scalpel, clean only for a moment before the torrent of hot blood erupts and spills over the son and snow. It steams, billowing clouds wafting up into the night as the body falls with a thump.

Tynan observes. After a long moment of silence, the even tones of the good doctor's voice echo once more within the close quarters of the cull-de-sac, "for I, absent in body but present in spirit, have judged already concerning he who hath so done this deed..." The blood covered boy steps towards his savior and bows his head while the good doctor continues to speak.

"And does your penance lie there..." His eyes remain fixed upon something behind the boy's shoulders and with a gentle touch does the good doctor guide his disciple around. At the edge of the twilight, tucked away within the cul-de-sac, are the trash heaped steps to a small church. Long abandoned, but already in the good doctor's eyes is it reborn and filled with the life of a willing congregation.

Tynan looks down at his disciple, the good doctor's eyes unblinking and in no way warm, but still filled with terrible purpose.

"Father Hugh," Tynan names his disciple and can already see the dark within the boy's eyes twist into this new persona, "here do you find your new home and new purpose."

The newly reborn Father Hugh blinks once, glory beginning to shine forth. He speaks with trembling anticipation, "To who am I to serve within this sanctuary?"

A good question, the good doctor's lips twitch ever so slightly towards what could become a smile, but does not. "To the innocent."

Father Hugh turns and looks up to his savior, "innocent?"

Tynan's lips twitch subtlety in the opposite direction, this time towards what might be a frown. "Worry not, for this sanctuary shall not in any way oppose the tenants of the Angry Chair. For true innocence shall be found only within…"

The good doctor trails off, one delicate eyebrow rising in question. A test for his new, young disciple. Father Hugh nods with a feverish smile as he turns his gaze back upon the ruined church that he is to restore and finishes his savior's sentence, "children."

"Very good Father Hugh, now go forth and administer. I do believe your flock shall be forthcoming in all too short a time. They are very special and we do not wish for them to need wait for you or all could be lost."

And Hugh does indeed go forth.

And very soon they shall arrive.

And the good doctor foresees himself to be most pleased.

Seven Crows : 207 : Justin Killam

Much Love from Nova Scotia Canada
Justin Killam

Manufactured by Amazon.ca
Bolton, ON